Mustang Mountain

Night Horse

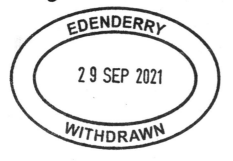
Sharon Siamon

Other Mustang Mountain titles:

Mustang Mountain

Night Horse

Sharon Siamon

EGMONT

EGMONT

We bring stories to life

To Reid

I wish to thank Dr Wayne Burwash, an equine practitioner who lives near Calgary, for his advice on equine injuries and recovery.

Night Horse first published by Walrus Books,
an imprint of Whitecap Books 2002
This edition published 2009
by Egmont UK Limited
239 Kensington High Street
London W8 6SA

Text copyright © 2002 Sharon Siamon
Cover photography © blickwinkel / Alamy
© Brian Bevan / Ardea
© Stephen Strathdee
© Paul Sisul
© Plush Studios
© Mark Andersen
© Mike Norton
© Visions of America, LLC / Alamy
© Tom Fullum

The moral rights of the author have been asserted

ISBN 978 1 4052 4308 7

1 3 5 7 9 10 8 6 4 2

A CIP catalogue record for this title is available
from the British Library

Typeset by Avon DataSet Ltd, Bidford on Avon, Warwickshire

Printed and bound in Great Britain by the CPI Group

CONTENTS

Chapter 1

Lost Luggage

'Where's my bag?' Meg O'Donnell stared at the ramp above the airport luggage carousel. The last suitcase slid down the ramp. The final passenger grabbed his luggage and hurried away. Meg was left, watching the carousel going around and around.

Meg's two friends, Alison Chant and Becky Sandersen, twirled their full luggage carts impatiently.

'I should go and look for my dad.' Becky's rosy cheeks were bright with excitement. 'He must be wondering where we are!'

'I'll come with you.' Alison thrust her cart through the crowd after her cousin Becky. 'Meg, you stay here and watch for your suitcase!'

'As if I could leave!' Meg shouted after them, but Becky and Alison were giggling and running with their piled-high luggage carts, pushing through the doors that led to the international arrivals area of the Calgary airport.

The carousel was almost empty now. Only a few lonely suitcases spun slowly around. Watching them, Meg felt like lost luggage herself. She tugged her long brown ponytail tight. Why had she let Alison talk her into coming to Mustang Mountain Ranch when she didn't want to be there – when she wanted to be home training Silver?

Meg thought of the beautiful three-year-old

colt standing alone in the paddock. She wished she were there right now, stroking Silver's soft mane, offering him a carrot. He wasn't actually her horse, but he had been given to her to gentle and train until it was time for his serious education as a jumper. She hated to waste a second of their precious time together.

Meg glared at the empty ramp as if she could make her grey and blue duffel bag magically appear. What if it never came? What if she just turned around and flew home?

Why had Alison insisted she come to the Mustang Mountain for the summer? Meg wondered. She didn't belong at the ranch like Becky and Alison. Becky lived there, when she wasn't going to school in the east. Her parents, Dan and Laurie Sandersen, ran the ranch. Alison was Becky's first cousin. As for herself – she was just Meg – Alison's almost invisible friend.

She saw Alison and Becky now, hurrying towards her. Becky's blonde hair floated around her happy, heart-shaped face. Alison, as usual, looked perfect, her dark hair smoothly in place, her clothes neatly pressed even after hours in a plane.

Becky's dad was with them. He was a tall, skinny cowboy who looked like someone who spent most of his life working outdoors.

'Hi, Meg,' he shook her hand shyly. 'You sure have grown up this year. I wouldn't have recongised you!'

'Hi, Mr Sandersen.' Meg suddenly felt shy. She knew she had grown over the winter – almost six inches! But she hated it when people made a fuss about the way she looked.

'Any sign of your lost suitcase?' Dan Sandersen finally stopped staring at her and scanned the circling carousel.

'Nope,' Meg shook her head.

'I don't see why it matters if you don't get your luggage,' Alison laughed. 'There's nothing in it but a bunch of baggy old sweatshirts and three pairs of leggings. That's all you ever wear!'

Meg winced. She had never realised what Alison thought of her clothes.

'You can borrow stuff from me until your suitcase shows up,' Becky said. 'We're almost the same size.' She tossed back her honey-blonde hair.

'But the picture I made for your mom was in there,' Meg said. She had done a pencil drawing of Windy, Laurie Sandersen's favourite horse. She had wanted to give it to Laurie as a gift when she arrived. It showed Windy, a sturdy little chestnut mare, galloping over the mountain meadow above the ranch.

'I'll see what I can find out about your suitcase.' Dan Sandersen shoved back his big cowboy hat. 'But we can't afford to wait around. We have to get up to the ranch before dark and it's a long drive and a long ride, as you remember.'

He strode away to the lost luggage department.

As she watched him go, Meg remembered the exciting ride to Mustang Mountain a year ago. She had been so thrilled that Alison had actually asked her to spend the summer on a real ranch in the Rocky Mountains. But that was last year. This summer, everything had changed.

Chapter 2

ROAD TO THE RANCH

Two hours later, riding along the old wagon road that led to Mustang Mountain Ranch, Becky Sandersen found herself breathless with excitement. She hadn't been home for the whole school year – almost ten months.

During that time she'd discovered how lucky she was to have parents like Laurie and Dan. Alison's mother and father fought constantly, and living with them had been tense and unhappy. Glancing at her dad, riding beside her, Becky smiled. Dad looked great, the same as ever. But how was her mother?

Last summer a big pack horse had kicked Laurie Sandersen while she was shoeing him, fracturing her spine. When Becky left for school her mother's back was just starting to heal and she was walking with a cane.

As they came around the last dusty bend, there was her mom, a small figure in jeans and a cowboy hat, waiting at the ranch gate. Becky rode ahead of the others, threw herself off her horse and vaulted over the gate.

Laurie enveloped Becky in a tearful hug. 'It's so good to have you back!'

Riding behind, Meg saw a shadow cross Becky's face as she hugged her mother. Laurie looked tired and she was still limping. She wasn't completely healed, not yet.

This isn't going to make Becky love horses any

more, Meg thought. Although Becky lived on a wilderness ranch and had ridden since she could walk, she didn't really like horses. She'd been bucked off when she was four and the terrifying memory had stayed with her.

'I have a big surprise for you,' Laurie Sandersen said, after she had greeted the other girls. 'I know you're tired, but I can't wait to show you . . . it's over here, in the foaling barn.'

As they walked towards the long low foaling barn, Meg drank in the sights and sounds of Mustang Mountain Ranch. She took a deep breath of the clean mountain air and felt it all the way to her toes. Despite missing Silver like crazy, she had to admit it was good to be back.

Laurie opened the barn doors and the three girls blinked, getting used to the dim light. Curious noses poked out of stalls, and the sound of steady munching came from hay nets hung where the mares could reach them.

In the first stall stood a small chestnut horse.

Her head was down, her eyes half-closed. She was dozing. Her belly was swollen with a foal, soon to be born.

'Mom!' Becky cried. 'That looks like Windy!'

'I'm afraid it is Windy,' Laurie said. 'Her foal is due any time.'

'I thought you weren't going to breed her for years. You were going to train her for endurance rides.' Becky glanced at her mother's worried face.

'That mustang stallion she met last summer had other ideas,' Laurie stroked her mare's soft nose.

'You mean Wildfire?' The three girls stared.

Visions of a wild red horse with a long flowing mane and tail filled Meg's imagination. Windy had run with his band for several days late last summer. And now she would be the mother of his foal.

As they walked back across the ranch yard, the sun was setting over the peaks of the Rockies.

On this ranch, high in a wilderness wildlife area, the government bred and trained horses for mountain patrols.

There were no cars, trucks or motorised vehicles allowed in the area, so all the patrolling was done on horseback. And the mountain horses had to be a very special breed – strong and able to climb steep trails littered with rocks, roots and fallen trees. They had to swim rivers and wade stony creek beds.

Windy's foal, Meg thought, would be a perfect mountain horse.

Lights blinked on in the ranch house, filling the yard with a cosy glow.

'Dinner in half an hour,' Laurie Sandersen told them. 'You've just got time to unpack and settle in your bunkhouse first.'

'Poor Meg, nothing to unpack,' Alison sang out. 'Come on, I want to get changed for dinner. I'm going to wear my new boots.'

'Are you dressin' up for the ranch hands?'

Becky teased. 'That scuzzy bunch will fall off their chairs!'

'Dressin' up?' Alison laughed at her cousin. 'You got your western drawl back awfully fast.'

Becky's light brown eyes sparkled. 'It just feels so good to be home.' The two of them ran laughing to a small bunkhouse set off to one side of the main ranch house.

'Dressing up,' Meg muttered, as she slowly followed the other two. 'That's a good one!' Why did Alison have to rub it in that Meg had no suitcase, or that her clothes were so much better? Alison's tooled leather cowboy boots had been a fourteenth birthday present from her parents. They had cost a fortune and made Alison look two inches taller.

Meg was hit by another wave of loneliness as she reached for the bunkhouse door. All summer, shut up in this little place with Alison! Lately, Alison had picked on her for every little thing and Meg didn't know why.

It had been bad enough being ignored. Now it seemed she couldn't do anything right.

Chapter 3

CHANCE

Three days later, Alison was holding her nose as she marched up and down the bunkhouse floor.

'Meg, take off those clothes and wash them or I'll rip them off you myself!' she exploded. 'You've been wearing the same clothes since we left New York. They stink!'

'It's none of your business,' Meg flared. 'I can wear these clothes all summer if I want.

Anyway, my bag could arrive today.'

'Who is going to ride two and a half hours
from the end of the road over a rough mountain
trail to deliver your suitcase?' Alison threw up
her arms. 'Nobody, that's who!'

'I can lend you some jeans and a shirt if you
want, Meg.' Becky held out a pair of blue jeans,
a white sleeveless T-shirt and a checked blue
flannel shirt. 'Your legs are longer than mine but
your boots should cover the gap.'

The breakfast bell interrupted them. The cook's
assistant struck the big steel triangle hanging
from the ranch house verandah with a metal
spoon, filling the quiet mountain air with a
harsh jangle.

'I'm starving, let's go!' Alison cried. Becky and
Alison were already dressed, ready to head for
the big low ranch house and a long table full of
flapjacks and maple syrup, sausages and
scrambled eggs, hot tea and fresh muffins.

Meg swallowed, thinking of breakfast. The

mountain air gave them all monstrous appetites. 'Just leave your clothes on my bunk,' she told Becky. 'I'll be there in a minute.'

The other two banged through the screen door and she heard their footsteps running across the hard-beaten dirt of the ranch yard.

Meg sighed. She supposed she'd have to give in. Her clothes did smell. She tugged her sweatshirt over her head and quickly pulled on the borrowed T-shirt to hide the bumps on her chest. Alison wore a bra and bragged about it. Meg just wished her body had stayed the way it was, maybe not beautiful, but comfortable. This new, taller self felt awkward and unfamiliar, as if she was in someone else's skin.

She pulled on Becky's stiff denim jeans, stood up and zippered them. She shrugged quickly into the checked shirt. It wasn't as big as she liked, but she could button it.

There was a full-length mirror on the back of the bathroom door. Meg took one look and slammed the door shut. Disaster! She wasn't going out there looking like that! The jeans were too tight, the shirt was too short – when she walked into the ranch house all the ranch hands would make dumb comments!

She'd rather starve.

Meg ran for her bunk, threw herself face down and wished for the thousandth time she were home. What she was doing here?

If she were home she'd be grooming Silver, watching him frisk around the paddock, just hanging out in the stable with him. Horses were so much more predictable than people, more loyal, more fun.

At that moment the world outside the bunkhouse exploded with sound. Meg jumped off her bunk as if she'd been shot and yanked back the curtain on the window above her bunk. She could see ranch hands running from the main house toward the barns. Other men stumbled from their bunkhouses, still pulling on their boots. They raced for the main corral where the mares and their foals were kept. The ruckus was over there.

Meg reached for her riding boots, struggled into them and burst out of the bunkhouse. She could hear the shouts of the men.

'It's that rogue mustang stallion!'

'He's after the mares!'

'He's kicking down the gate – get your ropes.'

The sound of thudding hooves and splintering wood was like crackling gunfire in the clear mountain air.

'Stay back, Miss. That horse is dangerous . . .!'

It was Slim, one of the oldest ranch hands at Mustang Mountain. Slim spat at the ground as he and Meg hurried towards the corral. 'That miserable mustang caught us with our pants down, this time. No time to saddle our horses, nothin'!'

Meg could see Wildfire now, a fury of pounding hooves, the colour of sunrise, the colour of fire. A final blow and the gate was shattered. Wildfire was through, a spinning, raging force, circling the mares.

Wildfire was the most beautiful horse Meg had ever seen. He had the proud arched neck, the prancing stride and the long flowing mane and tail of the true wild stallion.

The ranch hands struggled to get a rope on that massive neck. One rope, two, three zinged through the air, but Wildfire was expert at dodging ropes. Meg heard him give a scream of command and saw him gallop back through the smashed gate.

Two of the mares streaked behind him, both with foals running at their heels. They were heading for the creek and the mountain meadow beyond.

It was too late to saddle horses and follow them.

And then, out of the corner of her eye, Meg saw a dark rider on a grey horse riding at a slant towards the mares, twirling a lasso that fell neatly over the lead mare's neck. It broke her stride as sharply and brutally as if she'd hit a wall. She went down and the rider in black tossed the rope to a ranch hand and rode after the second mare.

His rope sang through the air. The second mare fell with the same force, and this time the strange rider threw himself out of the saddle and secured the struggling horse himself.

Becky and Alison came running up. Becky was jumping up and down. 'He got them. He saved the mares!'

The cowboy mounted his grey horse and rode up to the corral fence. He wore a black felt cowboy hat with a braided cord, a black shirt and leather chaps over his jeans. He tipped his hat to the three girls and they saw his hair was pale, like fine straw, and his eyes hazel, a kind of yellow green.

Beside her, Meg could almost feel Alison melting into the fence rail. 'Nice riding,' Alison said. She tried to put on her confident, mature voice, but Meg could hear the quaver in it.

The cowboy in black ignored her. His eyes were fixed on Meg. 'I just happened to be riding by at the right time, I guess,' he said. 'My name's Chance Williams. Who would you be?'

Meg almost turned around to see who he was talking to and then in a rush realised he meant her. He was asking her! Lately, men had been paying attention to her like this. It made her nervous and awkward.

'I'm M-Meg O'Donnell,' she stammered. 'And this is Alison Chant and Becky Sandersen. Becky's parents are the ranch managers.'

'That's fine,' Chance said. He had a slight southern drawl. 'Would you three young ladies know anything about that horse?'

He pointed up the mountainside, where Wildfire was a swiftly moving blur of red.

'We know everything about him,' Alison began eagerly. 'We call him Wildfire.'

Just then Dan and Laurie Sandersen hurried up to the fence.

'Thanks very much,' Dan said, shaking Chance's hand. 'Good piece of roping.'

'Can we invite you to breakfast?' Laurie asked. 'You must have been on the trail early.'

'Yes, I surely was, Ma'am.' Chance gave a wide grin that seemed to split his face. He looped his horse's reins over the fence. 'Breakfast sounds fine.'

'Isn't he dreamy?' Alison swooned as they followed Chance and Becky's parents back to the ranch house.

'Here you go again,' Becky groaned. 'I thought it was Jesse that was the hottest guy in the world.'

The summer before Alison had had a terrible crush on Jesse, the head ranch hand at Mustang Mountain. She'd been disappointed to find out that he was away from the ranch, taking an equine management course in Montana.

'Jesse's just a kid,' Alison said scornfully. 'Chance is a real man!'

Meg reached up and twisted her hair into a ponytail. She had run out of the bunkhouse without an elastic or clip to hold it off her face. 'I'm going back to the bunkhouse,' she mumbled.

'No, come on and have breakfast,' Becky smiled. She draped an arm over Meg's shoulder. 'Your hair looks good down like that – and you look fine in my clothes.'

'Did you see the way he rode?' Alison was still gazing after Chance.

Meg stopped and stared after the tall cowboy. 'I saw,' she said slowly. 'I didn't like the way he roped those mares. It was too rough – he could have hurt them.'

'You're such a wuss,' Alison said scornfully. 'He got them back from Wildfire, didn't he?'

Meg shook her head. 'There's something weird about the way Chance just happened to be there at exactly the right time, with two ropes coiled and ready to go on his saddle horn.'

The conversation at breakfast table was all about Wildfire.

'That mustang stallion has been causing nothing but trouble all winter,' Dan Sandersen told Chance, who was sitting across the long plank table from him. 'We didn't see him much up here at the ranch – he spent the winter down on the range where the grazing was better. The ranchers didn't take too kindly to him stealing their mares. I heard a couple of them tried to take a shot at him.'

'Can they shoot a wild mustang?' Meg put down her fork and stared at Becky's dad.

'They can in Alberta – if he's on private property.' Dan nodded. 'Up here, of course, he's protected. No one is allowed to shoot any animal on the wildlife preserve.'

Laurie Sandersen came over to join the conversation. 'That horse is a menace,' she groaned. 'Last summer he got my best mare with foal.'

Becky gave her mother a worried glance. Anything that upset Laurie upset her. 'Isn't there some way to stop Wildfire?' she asked.

'We could catch him and ship him off to a mustang preserve,' Dan said, 'but horses like Wildfire are almost impossible to rope. And some of them would rather die than lose their freedom.'

Meg shuddered. 'But it seems so awful to shoot a wild horse. How could anyone do that?'

Chapter 4

SURPRISE AT THE STREAM

Meg caught Chance's look from across the table. His pale eyes seemed to be boring into hers, and she twisted uncomfortably. For some reason she thought of the two helpless mares, brought up short at the end of his rope.

'I'll be going now.' He stood up and tipped his hat to Laurie Sandersen. 'Thanks for your hospitality.'

'I hope we'll see you again,' Laurie said politely. 'Will you be in the area long?'

'I don't think so, Ma'am. I'm just up here to do some back country riding and get away from civilisation for a while.' He bowed at the three girls. 'A pleasure to make your acquaintance.' He gave Meg a special nod and she found herself turning away impatiently.

The three of them followed him outside.

'Oooh, isn't he fabulous,' Alison sighed as they watched Chance Williams ride away.

'Did you see the way he was lookin' at Meg?' Becky giggled. 'I'd say she made a definite impression on him.'

'Stop it.' Meg kicked at the dirt. 'I don't like him somehow. He's too old to be staring at fourteen-year-olds and too smooth, like a TV cowboy.'

'Oh, Meg!' Alison turned on her. 'What's the matter with you? You're always so mousy where men are concerned.' She gave Meg a sharp look.

'He was probably just teasing. He couldn't be seriously interested in a girl like you.'

Becky laughed. 'But I suppose he could take you seriously, is that it?'

'Well, and why not?' Alison demanded. Her dark eyes snapped. 'I'm more mature looking than you, and much more than Meg.'

'Leave me out of this conversation!' Meg was suddenly furious with both of them. 'I'm going for a ride.' She ran towards the barn, Alison's insult ringing in her ears. Mousy!

'Want company?' Becky called after her.

'No!' Meg bellowed back. 'I want to go on my own!'

Alison shrugged her slim shoulders as she watched Meg streak away. 'Why is she so touchy?'

'Why do you give her such a hard time?' Becky laughed.

'I don't know, she just gets on my nerves,' Alison grumped. 'Meg's different lately.'

'Sure, she's grown six inches. And have you noticed how great she looks in my jeans?'

'Lumpy old Meg? With her hair all over the place and no make-up? You must be kidding.' Alison's dark eyebrows shot up in surprise.

'Lumpy? She doesn't look lumpy to me. And some people don't need make-up.' Becky grinned at her cousin. It was so easy to tease Alison, to get her going. And Becky was glad to see Meg getting some of her own back. Alison was used to treating her friend like some kind of loyal puppy that would always be at her heel no matter what. She didn't seem too happy at all the new attention Meg was getting.

A few minutes later, Meg was riding up the mountain meadow, urging her horse Brownie to put some distance between herself and the ranch.

Brownie wasn't fast. He was a typical

mountain horse, with strong legs and large feet, built for riding over the roughest trails. He could go for hours at a walk, but loping up a meadow was not his style.

Meg got off after a while, and stood looking down at the ranch. It looked so beautiful, nestled in the valley. Meg felt her stormy spirits calm at the sight. The peaks rose in a circle around her, glistening with snow. The grass under her feet was lush and green and dotted with flowers of every colour.

She had almost forgotten how much she loved this place. If only Alison were not such a pain!

She led Brownie to the edge of the meadow, through a screen of poplars to a small stream where he could drink.

The sun filtering through the leaves on the trees made dancing spots of light on the water and Brownie's smooth brown coat. Meg sat down on a rock to let him drink his fill.

A moment later, Brownie jerked up his head,

swivelling his ears forward. Another horse was coming downstream.

Meg could hear its hooves clopping on the rock. Then there was silence. Meg sat very still hoping whoever it was would go away.

She could hear singing. It was soft and low and in another language. Then there were splashing sounds, and laughter. This wasn't Chance, or anyone from the ranch.

Feeling curious, but a bit afraid, Meg slid from her rock and moved slowly upstream, leading Brownie.

Around the bend in the stream was a rock pool. A young man and a horse were wading in the pool. The horse was an Appaloosa, with dark spots over a white body. The young man had long black hair, braided down his back. He wore a red checked shirt and faded blue jeans.

While Meg watched he bent to drink from a waterfall at one side of the stream, where the water would be purest and freshest, absorbing oxygen as it bubbled over the rocks. The horse drank too.

Then they clambered on to the far bank. The young man bent over and picked up something from the ground.

'Palouse,' she heard him say. 'I have a gift for you. It will make you run as fast as an eagle can fly.'

Meg watched in fascination as the young man rested his forehead on the forehead of his horse, speaking to him softly and gently. He moved all around the horse, stroking his mane, his shoulder and flanks, his legs and belly. Then he began to braid the eagle feather into the mane of the horse.

Meg longed for her sketch book and pencil. This young man could be an Aboriginal hunter of long ago, preparing his horse for a buffalo hunt or a battle. Meg held her breath – they seemed so perfect, so beautiful she felt shivers run through her.

'There!' the young man said. 'Now we go on with our search. And when we need to fly, Palouse, you'll be ready.'

The horse nickered and rested his head on the young man's shoulder for a moment. Then the young man seemed to float up through the air, landed on the horse's bare back, and rode off upstream.

Chapter 5

MY HORSE, MY FRIEND

For a second Meg stood entranced. This was how she wanted to train Silver – this was the kind of relationship she wanted with her horse – close as a sister, or a best friend. She had to find out more about that young man.

She snapped to attention. The remarkable young man and his horse were disappearing, and if she didn't hurry she might never see him again!

She climbed on Brownie's back and urged him forward. Occasionally she would get glimpses of the Appaloosa's spotted hide, moving in and out among the dappled patches of sunlight. Where were they heading? She was too shy to ride up beside them, and anyway, the Appaloosa moved more quickly than Brownie. Still, he kept just in sight. Sometimes she'd think she'd lost him around a bend in the creek, and then she would hear his hooves splashing through the shallow water as he crossed the stream, and see a flash of white hide, or the boy's red plaid shirt.

Around a last bend, Meg stopped in amazement. There was the Mustang Mountain Ranch, right ahead of them. She had never come to it from this angle before.

The young man had stopped his horse too. He turned in his saddle and was laughing at her.

Meg wanted to ride off in the opposite direction as fast as Brownie's sturdy legs could take them, but she also wanted badly to find out more about this person and the way he handled horses.

She kept going, until he was close enough to call out, 'Are you part horse?'

'What do you mean?' The extraordinary question made Meg forget her shyness.

'You did just what horses often do. They're curious about you, so they follow, the way you did, but they don't come up to you asking lots of questions.'

'Are you a Native horse gentler?' Meg asked bluntly. It was time for questions.

'No, I'm not a full-blood Indian, and I don't gentle horses for a living,' the young man laughed again.

He was even better looking close up than at a distance. His teeth were even and white in a tanned face, his eyes so solid brown Meg couldn't see the pupils. His long braid was black and shiny.

'My name's Thomas Horne,' the young man

said. 'I ranch with my grandfather up near Rocky Mountain House. We lost our stallion and we can't afford to buy another good one. I read about a sorrel mustang stallion over this way on the Internet – so I came looking for him.'

'You read about Wildfire on the net?' Meg's head was whirling.

'Yup, on the wild horse website. The ranchers in the valley are pretty upset about this stallion taking their mares. I've heard they even hired a Wyoming bounty hunter to shoot him for twenty-five thousand dollars.'

Meg stared at him. 'They hired someone to kill Wildfire!' She was horrified. 'That would be murder!'

'You seem to know all about this horse I'm looking for. I guess I've come to the right place.' Thomas gestured towards the ranch. 'Is this where you live?'

'Yes, I mean, no. I'm just visiting for the

summer. My friend's parents train mountain patrol horses here for the government. Wildfire's been hanging around for two summers.'

'So you've seen him?' Thomas gave her an eager look from under his straight black brows.

'Lots. He's beautiful! He was here this morning, kicking down a fence to get at the breeding mares.' Meg took a deep breath and urged Brownie closer to Thomas's horse. 'It's really not my place to ask you, but I'm sure the people who run the ranch would like to hear about that bounty hunter.'

She couldn't let him just ride away, Meg thought, blushing at her sudden interest in this boy. He seemed closer to her own age than she had thought. How had he come to know so much about horses? And it wasn't just the way he handled them she liked, it was everything about him, the way he looked, the way he talked and moved. She suddenly had the horribly embarrassing thought that she was glad she was wearing Becky's tight jeans and shirt, not her old, sloppy sweats.

'Well, then, lead the way.' Thomas held Palouse back while Meg rode ahead towards the ranch.

Chapter 6

NIGHT
WATCH

Thomas was welcomed at the Mustang Mountain
Ranch. After a few minutes with Becky's father,
Meg was pleased to see them deep in
conversation about breeding horses for mountain
use. Laurie Sandersen wanted to pick his brain
about training horses for endurance rides. They
talked about Wildfire, and how Thomas wanted
him to be the foundation of his herd.

That night, there was a campfire in the ranch yard.

The campfire site was a large shallow pit, lined with round river stones. Logs were set around it as seats, and the firelight danced high in the air. The tall black coffeepot sat right on the burning logs, letting out a thin trickle of steam.

Tonight they were expecting Windy's foal to be born. Everyone on the ranch had agreed to take a shift watching the young mare. They sat around the fire, their faces bright in the light of the flames, the rest of the ranch in darkness. The talk and laughter was warm like the fire's glow.

Meg's eyes never left Thomas's face. She liked his high cheekbones and the grooves around his mouth. She liked the way he didn't say much, but when he did people listened, even though he was so young. He told them about the bounty hunter looking for Wildfire.

'Dirty rotten skunk,' Slim, the old ranch hand,

growled. 'Taking money for shooting a horse like that!'

'I think Chance Williams might be the bounty hunter,' Meg whispered to Alison.

'You're crazy,' Alison huffed. 'Just because you didn't like him doesn't mean he shoots wild horses for money!' The firelight glinted dangerously in her eyes. 'I suppose Thomas Horne is more your style. He is cute . . .' she whispered, nudging Meg's arm.

'Shut up! He's not cute,' Meg whispered furiously back. She refused to let Alison drag Thomas down into her collection of cute boys – he was so much more than that!

'I really hope Windy is going to be a great endurance horse,' Laurie Sandersen was saying to Thomas. 'I wasn't going to breed her for a few years. I hope having a foal so young doesn't hurt her chances.'

'It shouldn't. Would you mind if I took a look at her?' Thomas asked.

'No. Come along.' Laurie stood up. 'It's time I checked on her, anyway.'

Laurie switched on the low-powered light in the foaling barn. Windy pricked up her ears at the sound of Laurie's voice but stood at the back of her stall, shifting her weight from one foot to another.

Meg, Becky and Alison stood quietly as Laurie entered the stall.

Meg could sense Thomas standing behind her. He seemed to communicate directly, without touch or word. She could feel his mind connecting with hers.

The little chestnut mare pawed at her bedding and looked back at her belly. It was so swollen she looked barrel-shaped.

Meg was filled with pity for the little horse. This was the lively mare she'd sketched frisking across a sunny meadow! It seemed too soon for

Windy to be a mother. She looked puzzled and unhappy.

'Her time is near,' Thomas said in a gentle voice. 'If she has an easy time she'll be fine. She looks strong.'

'I know, that's why I want to be here when the foal is born, so I can help if she has trouble.' Laurie stroked Windy's face lovingly. 'I'll take the first watch. I'll wake you three around five and you can watch until sunrise,' she told the girls. 'Go and get some sleep now.'

It felt raw and damp at five in the morning. The mountains were hidden in thick mist.

Meg hadn't slept well – she'd been thinking about Thomas. She hardly noticed the strange feeling of pulling on Becky's cold stiff jeans. Would he still be here?

'Has Windy's foal been born?' Becky croaked, still hoarse with sleep.

'No.' Laurie Sandersen looked worried. 'Not yet. Thomas is watching her. Grab some breakfast and go take over.'

Thomas was here – at the foaling barn. Meg couldn't wait to see him. They ate cold cereal in the ranch house kitchen and ran shivering to the barn.

Thomas was sitting cross-legged on a blanket on a pile of hay. He looked relaxed, but alert. 'Still nothing.' He stood up and stretched his arms over his head. 'I think she'll wait until tomorrow night.'

Meg was so glad to see him she didn't even glance at Windy. 'Will you stay?' she asked.

Thomas shook his head. 'I'd better go and find my stallion,' he smiled.

'You'll break Meg's heart if you just ride away.' Alison gave him a flirtatious smile.

'S-stop it,' Meg stammered, burning with embarrassment. She'd never forgive Alison for this! 'It's nothing like that. I'm training a horse,' she tried to explain. 'I want to be as close to him as you are to Palouse. I need to learn how to do it.' There. She had spoken her heart's desire. She waited for Thomas to laugh at her, but he only nodded.

'Why do mares wait 'til the middle of the night to drop their foals?' Becky yawned. 'That's what I want to know.'

'Because in the wild a mare is the most vulnerable when she's giving birth,' Thomas told her. 'She wants to be hidden and alone – it's instinct.'

He smiled at Meg. 'I'll drop in and see how things are going before I head back to our ranch,' he promised. 'Good luck with Windy.' Then he disappeared into the faint dawn light.

Meg sat down with a thump on the blanket. It was still warm from his body. For some reason she felt like crying.

'Well,' Alison yawned. 'What do we do now?'

'Huddle here and keep each other warm,'

Becky snuggled in beside Meg, 'and wait for Windy to have her baby.'

'Well I hope she hurries up.' Alison plopped down beside them. 'I want to go back to bed!'

Alison's yawns were catching. Becky yawned so hard her jaws seemed to creak. 'Whatever we do, we have to stay awake!' she said. 'Prop your eyelids open – anything – but we can't fall asleep!'

Becky's warning worked in reverse. The harder Meg tried to stay awake, the more her eyelids drooped. She tried thinking about Thomas – the way she had seen him on the riverbank with Palouse, braiding an eagle feather into his mane. Then Palouse turned a glorious golden red and his neck was arched like a stallion, and his tail almost swept the ground. Chance was hiding in the shadows with a gun. 'Wake up!' Meg tried to scream with all her strength, but no sound came out . . .

'Wake up, wake up!' Laurie was shaking her shoulder.

'Mom, what's happened? Did Windy have her foal?' The three of them sat bolt upright staring at Laurie Sandersen's frightened face.

'No,' Laurie said. 'She's gone!'

Chapter 7

SEARCH FOR WINDY

The three girls sprang to their feet. The door to Windy's stall was wide open. There was no sign of her.

'How did she get out?' Becky rubbed her eyes.

'Her stall was unlatched,' Laurie Sandersen was examining the door. 'There's no way she could open it herself. Did you see anyone, or hear anyone come into the barn?'

'No.' They glanced at each other, ashamed.

'The truth is, all three of you were sound asleep.' Laurie's face was full of anger and pain. 'Someone could have walked right in here and taken Windy, and you wouldn't have known.'

'I wasn't that much asleep,' Becky defended herself. 'I had one ear open for Windy.'

'Then someone was careless and left the stall unlatched,' Laurie was pacing up and down. 'Did you check it before you all collapsed in a heap on the hay?'

Miserably they shook their heads.

'Who was in here before you?' Laurie asked.

'Thomas!' Meg blurted. 'But he wouldn't have left the stall unlatched.'

She could see suspicion dawning on the three faces in front of her.

'Unless he wanted her to escape,' Alison said. 'Windy would be excellent bait to catch Wildfire. All he'd have to do is follow her and wait for Wildfire to show up.'

'No!' Meg shouted, her voice loud in the quiet barn. 'I know Thomas wouldn't do that!'

'But Thomas does want that stallion very badly,' Becky said slowly.

'So does Chance Williams,' Meg wanted to scream. But she had only her dream to back her up.

'You three should have checked the latch on the stall,' Laurie Sandersen said sternly. 'And you shouldn't have fallen asleep. I'm disappointed in all of you, and if anything happens to Windy . . .' She drew herself up taller and took a deep breath. 'Never mind. The important thing is to find her as quickly as we can!' She banged the stall shut. 'I'll go and get some search parties organised.'

She limped away, leaving the three of them feeling lower than snakes' bellies.

'I'll tell you one thing,' Becky said in a low voice, clenching her fists, 'if I find the person who unlatched this stall and let Windy out

I'm going to personally take him apart.'

Meg knew it was her mom Becky was worried about, not Windy.

In the still dark bunkhouse they dressed for a day in the saddle – sweatshirts over long-sleeved shirts, rain gear to tie to the back of their saddles, hats to keep off the sun and sturdy riding gloves and boots.

Dawn was coming over Mustang Mountain as they ran to the barn. The mountain top looked like a wild horse, running, with ears pricked forward and long mane and tail flying.

The morning sun lit it like flames. 'Run, Wildfire,' Meg whispered to herself. 'Run as far and as fast as you can from this mountain!'

In the barn they tacked up along with the other ranch hands and Becky's father. Water bottles and quick, high-energy snacks went into their saddle bags. They rode geldings – mares might be unpredictable with a wild stallion in the neighbourhood.

'You be careful out there,' Dan Sandersen told them. 'Stay close to the ranch and let us do the long riding today.'

'I'll take Hank,' Becky told her father. She centred Hank's saddle blanket carefully. 'He's old and slow, but I can trust him.'

Watching Becky's skilled but uncaring hands saddle Hank, Meg felt sad. What a contrast to the way Thomas touched and handled his horse!

It always amazed Meg that Becky didn't like horses when she had been around them all her life. She knew that Becky's memories of being thrown from a horse as a little girl haunted her. Her mother's accident last summer hadn't helped. Becky had to ride at Mustang Mountain Ranch because no motorised vehicles were allowed up in the wildlife preserve, but she didn't love riding the way Meg did.

*

Their search took them up a ridge behind the ranch.

They stopped their horses on top of the ridge and looked over the whole valley.

'I wonder where Chance is now?' Alison sighed deeply. 'I wonder if he just rode away on his tall grey horse and I'll never see him again.'

'Something tells me you'll see Chance,' Meg muttered. She remembered his swift sure attack on the runaway mares. Chance Williams wouldn't give up easily on what he wanted.

'You still think Chance is after Wildfire!' Alison turned in her saddle and glared at Meg. 'Haven't you got the wrong guy? How about Thomas?'

'We're supposed to be looking for Windy, not some guy,' Becky said disgustedly. 'Meg, have you joined the boy-crazy club? I thought you were smarter than that.'

Meg urged Brownie forward. Becky's

accusation stung. It was true that Thomas filled her thoughts as no one ever had. She found herself going over every word, every look of their meeting the day before. She felt as if she could not stop moving until she found him again and they were talking and laughing together. These were such new feelings she couldn't put them into words. Could Becky be right? Was she getting as boy-crazy as Alison?

The valley below them was quiet in the morning light. 'There's no sign of Windy here,' Becky said. 'Let's keep ridin' in this direction.' She pointed north into a forested area.

The three girls combed dry gullies and stream beds where the trees grew thick and a mare could hide. They stopped and ate, and rode on again. Finally Alison called a halt. 'How long are we going to keep this up?' she groaned. 'We've been riding all day. I'm sore, and Sugar is limping.' Alison's horse, Sugar, was a light bay with a white blaze down his face.

Becky slid off Hank's back. 'I'm not goin' back until it gets dark or we find Windy,' she said wearily. 'Which foot is Sugar favouring?'

'The right forefoot,' Alison told her. 'We're not the only ones looking for Windy. What if somebody already found her?'

'Steady boy.' Becky picked up Sugar's foot and dug a stone out of the hoof. 'They'd fire off a shot to let us know. We haven't heard anything.' She straightened up and dusted her hands. 'There, Sugar should be OK, now. Are you two comin' with me, or do you want me to go on lookin' by myself?'

'Oh, we wouldn't dream of leaving you out here on your own,' Alison said sarcastically. 'We'll search all night if we have to!'

The shadows were getting long when they stopped again and dug another snack out of their saddle bags. 'What's over there?' Meg asked, pointing to a low, treeless area.

'It looks like a muskeg bog,' Becky said. 'The

ground looks solid, but it's just tufts of grass and moss floatin' on rotten black gooey stuff and water.'

'There's something moving near the edge.' Alison shaded her eyes to keep the long slanting rays of the sun out of them. 'See – what is that?'

They crumpled their chocolate bar wrappers and drink boxes, quickly stuffed them into their saddle bags and rode down a gentle slope and through a prickly stand of scrubby spruce trees to the bog.

They could hear grunting now, the sound of a horse in pain or trouble. Deep in the shadow was Windy, struggling to free herself from the sucking mat of rotting vegetation below her. She had sunk to her round belly, and the grunts were coming from deep in her throat.

Squatted on the shore was another figure, speaking quietly to the frantic mare. 'Come little girl, come out of there. Try. Try again.'

Thomas! Meg felt a thrill of joy and relief. Thomas was here!

As the girls watched, Windy made a gigantic effort to free herself. The sounds that came from her throat were terrible.

Meg felt shame flood through her. How could she feel happy to see Thomas when Windy was in such danger? She was a traitor!

'Get off your horses,' Thomas's calm quiet voice reached them clearly. 'Don't frighten her. She must not start thrashing around or she'll sink in deeper.'

'Poor Windy!' Alison said. 'We've got to get her out of there!'

Becky quietly dismounted and led Hank around the edge of the bog. 'Be careful where you put your feet,' she called back to Meg and Alison. 'It looks solid, but it's not. Try to stay close to the trees.'

'What happened?' Meg asked when they had finally worked their way around to

Thomas's side. 'Why is Windy here?'

'Mares often look for water when they give birth,' Thomas said. 'No one knows why, but perhaps they feel safer with water nearby. I've been here about half an hour. Before I came Windy must have struggled for hours. She's very tired.' He glanced up at them. 'How did she get out of the foaling barn?'

'As if you didn't know.' Alison stood with her hands on her hips. 'What are you doing here?'

'Trying to save Windy's life, and her foal's,' Thomas said calmly. 'But I'm afraid we're too late.'

'Couldn't you throw a rope around her neck and pull?' Meg asked desperately.

'She's stuck fast.' Thomas shook his head. 'Pulling on her neck will only make her struggle and sink deeper.'

'There must be something we can do!' Becky cried. 'You're supposed to be the horse expert – think of something!'

'Windy will have to free herself, if she can,' Thomas said. 'It is her struggle. But we can help by talking to her and concentrating with her.'

'You're nothing but a phony.' Alison glared at him. 'Concentrate, my foot! Let's go for help!'

Chapter 8

Wild Stallion at Dusk

'It's too far back to the ranch,' Becky moaned. 'Help won't come in time.'

'Let's try Thomas's way,' Meg urged. She squatted down beside him and focused her attention on Windy. 'Come on, girl,' she coaxed. 'You can do this.'

Windy gave a helpless whinny and lowered her head. She shook it from side to side in distress. Her sides were heaving and her ears drooped. Meg's heart went out to her. She should be standing in her nice warm stall, not stuck in a horrible bog. The smell of it was like rotten eggs.

Windy struggled and nickered in despair.

'There's nothing we can do –' Thomas started to say. Suddenly, there was a commotion in the trees to the left of them. A soft neigh answered Windy's call.

Thomas held up his hand. 'Be quiet, be still,' he whispered.

A shaft of late afternoon light came through a gap in the ragged spires of the spruce trees. Into it stepped Wildfire, so close to them that they could see his large, intelligent eyes and flaring nostrils.

He pawed the soft earth and whinnied to Windy again, then trotted a little closer with a high springing step, his proud neck arched high.

Meg took a deep breath. There was something

so wild and magnificent about Wildfire.

He was close enough now to see deep scars across his face. One had narrowly missed an eye. There were more scars on his strong withers, and rope burns around his neck. Wildfire looked like he had been in many battles since he led them through a forest fire the summer before. That's when he had first run Windy off to be part of his band.

Poor Windy! Meg turned to look at her and gasped. The change in Windy was amazing. Her head was up and her ears pricked forward. The dull, lifeless look was gone from her eyes.

Wildfire paced back and forth along the edge of the bog, his tail held high. He threw back his great head and gave a piercing whinny of command.

It was like he sent an electric shock through Windy.

She moved, first one foreleg, and then the other. She was making one last mighty effort to free herself.

'Come on, Windy, come on,' Meg urged under her breath, trying to throw all her powers of concentration behind the effort. 'You can make it – come on!'

Windy let out a groan, gave a great plunge, and then another. She was almost at the shore. Meg saw Thomas spring up and reach for a rope.

'I'm going to lasso her,' he cried. 'Help me hold her!'

Meg had a moment of rebellion. Windy didn't want to be held – she had made this tremendous effort so she could run free with Wildfire! That's where she wanted to be. She had fought for life to go with him.

But of course Thomas was right. Windy was going to have her foal and she was exhausted. Running free on the open range would have to wait. 'But I promise you,' Meg whispered fiercely. 'Someday you'll get your wish. You've earned it.'

The rope tightened around Windy's neck.

Alison, Becky and Meg helped Thomas hold the little mare as she staggered on to firm ground.

Wildfire nickered softly to her, paced around the bog, and then turned and galloped away into the setting sun.

They were all wet and covered with black bog dirt.

Thomas stroked Windy's nose and ran his hand over her belly. 'The foal is down in the birth position. It won't be long now,' he spoke to Meg, 'you must get her away from this place, and wipe her down. Massage her legs and back if she'll let you, and make sure she has clean water to drink.' He walked over to his horse and gathered Palouse's reins in his left hand.

'Where are you going?' Meg asked in surprise.

'I have to go after the stallion,' Thomas said. 'I'll be back if I can.'

He did his amazing leap on to Palouse's back and rode away through the trees without looking back.

'What a hero,' Alison said disgustedly. 'He just leaves us here with a half dead horse who is about to have a foal and rides away.' She wheeled on Meg. 'Now do you think Thomas is so wonderful? I'm sure he's the one who unlatched the foaling stall. His plan worked out perfectly. Wildfire came.'

'It will be dark soon.' Becky shivered. 'Whatever Thomas's reason for leaving us, we have to get Windy to a safe dry place, and get a fire goin'. Did you see those fresh scars on Wildfire's face? He's been fightin' with a cougar. The cougar is probably still around.'

Meg was still staring at the place where Thomas had disappeared. She had to admit he looked guilty. At the very least he was more interested in catching Wildfire than in helping them save Windy and her foal.

'I've been an idiot.' She yanked her ponytail tight. She was as bad as Alison with her TV cowboy. She'd been taken in by the image of the strong silent horse gentler. If this was how it felt to be crazy about somebody, Alison could have it!

Chapter 9

ALONE IN THE DARK

'Ugh! Let's get out of here,' Alison shivered. 'This bog is a spooky, smelly place.'

The scream of a hunting cat sent shivers down all their backs.

'What was that?' Meg moved closer to Windy and tried to soothe the frightened mare.

'A cougar,' Becky said. 'Maybe the same one that attacked Wildfire!' She urged Windy forward. 'Dad says foals are a cougar's favourite food! Let's go, girl – we'll start a fire that will keep that big cat away.'

As they worked their way up the slope, dragging and coaxing the exhausted young mare, Becky stopped to break spruce branches off the bottom of the trees. They were dry and full of spruce gum to help get a fire burning bright and hot.

Above the bog, in a small clearing, they found an overhanging ledge of rock. It curved around forming a three-sided natural shelter. The sun had baked the rocks all day and now they radiated stored heat.

'This will have to do,' Becky said. 'I don't think Windy can go any further.' Windy pressed close to the warm rock and a shudder went through her body.

'We'll need a lot of firewood to keep a fire going all night.' Meg looked around the clearing. 'Let's get moving – it will be dark soon!'

Meg, Becky and Alison fanned out from their shelter as the shadows grew deeper and the sun disappeared behind the mountain peaks above them.

They dragged scraggy dried pine branches and handfuls of small dead twigs to the rock shelter. They knocked over small dead trees to add to the pile.

'There!' Becky stood back eyeing the tangled heap of wood they had made. 'It's not pretty but it should last us 'til mornin'.'

Before they lit the fire they made a circle of stones, and scraped the loose soil away. It was no use starting a fire that would set the whole forest blazing.

'I've only got three matches,' Becky said, pulling an emergency kit out of her saddle bag. 'The fire has to start on the first one.'

Carefully, she built a tower of small spruce twigs, then stuffed paper from a chocolate bar down inside. Slightly bigger sticks, broken over her knee, went over the tower, like a log cabin. 'Break lots of these,' she told Alison and Meg, 'in case the first ones don't catch.' She squatted down and struck the first match on a rock. A gust of wind blew it out instantly.

'Stand over there and make a windbreak,' Becky said. 'I've only got two matches left. I want to save one, in case the fire goes out later.'

The second match blazed. Becky held it to the paper inside the tower. The paper smouldered, smoked, and then a tiny orange flame licked up and caught the spruce twigs. In seconds, the fire was blazing, and they were tossing on more sticks.

'Just small ones!' Becky said. 'And not too many at a time!'

'Absolutely brilliant,' Meg said as the cheery fire crackled and snapped. They crouched around it, letting the warmth dry out their damp bones. The darkness and loneliness retreated from the circle of brightness, making them all feel more cheerful.

Meg found herself thinking of Thomas's warm brown eyes. He'd be proud of how they'd managed. She shoved the thought away angrily. The three of them had done all this on their own. They didn't need Thomas, or anyone!

'We'll have to keep feedin' the fire,' Becky warned. 'Don't let it get too low.'

'And we need to see to our horses.' Meg stood up. They had left Hank and Sugar and Brownie saddled and bridled, tied with lead ropes to the trees.

'And get all this caked bog mud off poor Windy,' Alison sighed, going over to the exhausted horse. 'She looks so uncomfortable!'

'Do you think she'll drop her foal before morning?' Meg glanced at the mare.

Becky shrugged tiredly. 'Mom says no one can tell exactly, especially since it's Windy's first foal.'

Just then, from a ridge high above them, came a long haunting howl. More howls joined in, until the dusk seemed thick with the sound.

'What's that?' Alison hugged Becky in fear.

'Wolves,' Becky said quietly. 'That's the Skeleton River pack, gatherin' up on the ridge.'

'I suppose foals are their favourite food, too?' Alison asked.

'They're not fussy – any weak or wounded animal will do,' Becky said. 'Let's get some more wood on the fire. Bring me that big branch.'

'I can help you with that.'

A low voice spoke from the darkness outside the circle of firelight, and the large branch seemed to move on its own.

Then the tall lanky figure of Chance Williams came into the light. He was still wearing his big black hat and the black stubble of a day's growth darkened his face. In one hand he held the dead branch, in the other a powerful rifle.

Alison leaped up from the fire. 'Chance!'

'I saw the smoke just before dark and rode down to see who had lit a fire.' Chance glanced around the clearing, his pale eyes reflecting the orange glow of the flames. 'There's wolves up on the ridge. What are you girls doing all by yourselves out here?'

'Windy got stuck in the bog and she's going to have her foal any minute,' Alison said, throwing out her arms dramatically.

'Could you go to the ranch and tell my parents where we are?' Becky asked. 'We can't get Windy to move and we sure could use some help.'

'I could do that.' Chance nodded.

'Wouldn't it be better if you stayed right here and protected us?' Alison begged. 'There's a cougar around, besides the wolves, and you have your rifle.'

'He can't shoot anything – it's a wildlife refuge, remember?' Meg shook her head. 'Anyway, we're all right. We have enough firewood to last until morning.'

'The girl's right.' Chance gave Meg one of his penetrating looks from under the brim of his hat.

'I think I'd better ride back to the ranch. Folks will be awfully worried about you.'

He stood up, his eyes still fixed on Meg. The way he stared made her squirm. 'Keep that fire burning bright.' Chance tipped his hat and vanished into the darkness. They could hear the crackle of breaking twigs as he walked, the jingle of his spurs and his low command to his horse. Then the sounds faded away.

'Why does he always look at Meg when he talks to us,' Alison muttered. 'It's as if I don't even exist.'

Becky sighed. 'I don't know if you've noticed, dear cousin, but Meg is getting better looking by the day.'

'Don't worry, I'm not interested in Chance.' Meg's blue eyes were stormy. 'There's something creepy about him. And why is he carrying that rifle?'

'Self-protection?' Alison said in her most sarcastic voice. 'Fighting off cougars and wolves maybe? Honestly, Meg, you're such a baby sometimes.'

'It's a high-powered hunting rifle with a telescopic sight,' Meg fired back. 'The kind of gun a bounty hunter would use for shooting a horse from a distance.'

Becky had moved away from the fire to check on Windy. 'I don't care who or what Chance is, just so he sends help,' Becky cried. 'Look at poor Windy!'

Chapter 10

BY THE DYING FIRE

Windy was moving restlessly at the end of her rope, pawing the ground and kicking at her belly. She had backed herself into the corner of the rock shelter. Her neck was arched, her nostrils flared wide and she was breathing hard.

'Something's happening,' Alison cried.

'She wants to lie down,' Becky said. 'We have

to get her away from the rock so the foal has room to be born.'

They tugged at Windy's rope and managed to turn her sideways to the rock wall. Meg could feel her heart pounding – it was really going to happen. She had never seen anything being born, not even a kitten or a goldfish.

'Do you know what to do?' she asked Becky.

'Not really, but I've watched my mom helpin' some of the mares. The trouble is, Windy's so tired from fightin' her way out of the bog. And it's her first foal.' Becky lifted a worried face. 'All we can do is hope it's an easy birth.'

'Look at that!' Alison was standing behind Windy. 'When she lifts up her tail you can see something white.'

'That's the birth sac,' Becky said.

Meg took a look at the thin balloon-like sac protruding from Windy's hind end. She looked away quickly, feeling her stomach churn.

Windy lay down on the mossy ground.

'The sac's getting bigger.' Alison was peering closely at the ballooning fetal sac. 'This is so interesting.'

Windy staggered to her feet again and as she did so there was a great gush of fluid from the bag.

'Wow!' Alison stepped back from the burst of fluid. 'What on earth was that?'

'Her water broke,' Becky said eagerly. 'It means the foal is comin'.'

Meg had to sit down – everything was going black. She couldn't watch what was going on and she was furious with herself.

'Meg!' Becky called. 'Build up the fire. We're going to need lots of light over here.'

Meg stumbled to her feet, relieved to have something else to concentrate on beside the birth of the foal. She dragged some big logs back to the fire pit, and armfuls of small sticks. Carefully, the way she'd seen Becky do it, she built the fire to a brighter blaze.

'I see something!' Alison shouted. 'It looks like

the feet. Shouldn't the head come out first?'

'That's human babies,' Becky told her. 'Foals are born feet first. It's OK.'

Meg wished Alison would stop sounding so interested and excited and above all would stop describing every single thing that was happening!

She glanced over. Windy had flopped down again and she could see the foal's tiny feet, still wrapped in the birth sack. She quickly looked away, swallowing hard.

She had this horrible feeling she was going to throw up!

For a few minutes everything was quiet except for the odd grunt from Windy and the sound of the fire crackling and hissing. Meg rocked back and forth, hugging herself and wishing it was over. 'I can't be sick, I can't be sick,' she repeated to herself.

Becky came to pace in front of the fire. She went back and checked on Windy.

'Why isn't anything happening?' Alison said. 'Shouldn't something be happening?'

'Yes,' Becky said. 'The foal should be comin' out. But I think Windy's too weak to push its head through the birth canal. I think we're going to have to help her by pullin' the foal.'

Meg gulped. 'Wouldn't it be better to just let nature take its course?' she muttered. 'We might . . . injure something.'

'I don't know,' Becky wailed. 'But I do know that sometimes people have to help if the mare is small and the foal is big, or if the birth is takin' too long. Both Windy and the foal could die if we don't.'

'Come on then.' Alison was already kneeling in position, trying to get a grip on the slippery legs. 'What are we waiting for?'

Becky joined her. Meg sat on a stone by the fire, her eyes shut. What a terrible, terrible thing for Windy to go through. How did anything get born when it was this hard?

'It's coming,' Alison grunted, pulling hard. 'I can see the head.'

'Come on, Windy,' Becky groaned. 'Just help us a little.'

In her mind, Meg could sense Windy drifting away, too tired, much too tired . . .

Thomas's words came into her mind. 'Concentrate with her, talk to her.'

Meg straightened her back and made a picture in her mind of Windy splashing through the shallows of Skeleton Creek, racing up the meadow across from the ranch, kicking up her heels and munching mouthfuls of green grass.

'Grass, Windy,' she said silently, trying to speak to the horse's mind. 'Running. Rolling on your back in the sun.'

'Look, the head's coming, and the shoulders,' she heard Alison's excited cry. 'This is so great – oh, I can't believe it, it's amazing.'

'Here it comes,' cried Becky, 'a perfect little foal. Look at it!'

Meg heard a gentle nicker from Windy.

'They're touching noses,' Alison whispered. 'They're saying hello!'

Daring to look, Meg glimpsed Windy and her foal, lying nose to nose. Windy's baby was born and it was alive.

Alison and Becky were laughing and cheering and hugging each other for joy.

'What happens now?' Alison asked eagerly.

'I don't really know,' Becky said hesitantly. 'I think Windy's supposed to stand up to break the cord, and then lick the foal all over to dry her off, and try to get the foal to stand up too.'

Meg had to put her head down quickly between her knees. It wasn't over yet, there was more yucky stuff, umbilical cords, and blood.

'Come and look, Meg, she's a filly,' Becky said softly. 'A little girl, and she's so beautiful.'

Meg had never heard Becky talk this way about a horse. 'I'm coming,' she choked, but she couldn't get her legs to move.

Ten minutes later she was still sitting frozen in the same spot. It was as if her brain could no longer give orders to her body.

'There's no hurry,' she heard a low voice close to her say.

Meg's eyes snapped open. A pair of legs in faded blue jeans were standing in front of her.

Chapter 11

CHANCE TAKES AIM

'Thomas!' Meg looked up at his plaid shirt, his smiling face and long dark braid.

'Windy had her foal,' Thomas said gently. 'Congratulations.'

'I had nothing to do with it,' Meg moaned. 'I couldn't even watch!'

Thomas squatted down and took Meg's hand. 'I told you that you are part horse. You lived through the birth with Windy, and it was hard. You're too tired to move.'

'No, that's not why I can't move,' Meg shook her head. 'I'm just a chicken, too scared of the sight of blood and stuff to help.'

Thomas pulled her gently up by the hand. 'There's nothing to be scared of – come and look. You won't faint, I promise.'

They walked out of the bright firelight into the warm shadows by the rock where Windy lay with her foal.

Meg looked down. A damp small head with a white star on its forehead was lying close to Windy.

Thomas was right. It wasn't yucky. She was looking at a miracle – a new baby horse, so small and so new that Meg felt a lump in her throat.

'She's going to be flame red, like her father,' she said.

Alison glanced up at Thomas. 'Where did you come from?' Her dark eyes were scornful. 'And why did you leave just when we needed you?'

'You didn't need me.' Thomas gestured around the clearing. 'You did everything just right.'

'You didn't answer her question.' Becky looked up from stroking the foal's head. 'Where did you come from just now?'

Meg tossed another log on the fire while Becky and Alison waited for Thomas's answer. She didn't care where he'd come from – she was just glad he had come back.

'I followed Wildfire after Windy got out of the bog,' Thomas said. 'That bounty hunter is somewhere nearby so I was trying to get him to run as far and as fast away from here as he could. I might as well have tried to turn the wind. He ran all right, but he just led me in a big circle, right back to his family. He's not going to leave as long as that cougar is threatening!'

Alison and Meg exchanged glances. Meg could see that Alison wasn't sure whether to believe Thomas.

'How do you know the bounty hunter is around here?' Alison challenged him.

'We've been weaving in and out of each other's tracks for days.' Thomas's brown eyes were serious. 'We both want the horse, but he wants him dead, and I want him alive.'

'I don't care about Wildfire,' Becky said fiercely. 'I want to save this foal and Windy.' She was still cradling the foal's head on her lap. 'I can feel she's gettin' weaker by the minute!'

Thomas knelt down by Windy's head. 'The mare must get on her feet,' he said, 'but she's still too tired.'

'What can we do?' Becky asked.

'The foal needs to nurse and breathe more deeply, to move and stretch her muscles. But while we're waiting for Windy to gather her strength we can rub the foal down and get her dry.'

Becky stripped off her sweatshirt, pulled the little filly across her knees and rubbed her thin, bony body. Holding on to her was like trying to cradle an octopus – the filly seemed to have too many long skinny legs, thrashing in all directions.

'That's good,' Thomas laughed. 'The more she moves the better.'

'I need another sweatshirt . . .' Becky said. 'This one is already wet!'

'Oh, here!' Alison gave a sigh. 'It's my best all-cotton white sweatshirt, but go ahead. Use it.'

Meg peered into the darkness around the fire. 'You think Wildfire is out there?' she asked.

'I know it.' Thomas said. 'He must have smelled the cougar because the last few kilometres he ran like the wind. All horses hate the big cats but these two must be old enemies. Wildfire has the scars to prove it. They're both out there, somewhere.'

'Don't worry,' Alison told him. 'Chance went back to the ranch to get help. They should come soon.'

Thomas stood up, his face red in the firelight. 'Chance Williams was here?' he asked sharply.

'Yes,' Meg said. 'And he had a big rifle with him.'

'I don't believe Chance went to get help,' Thomas grunted. He strode over to Windy, who still lay stretched on her side. 'Come on, little horse, get up. You must move. There is danger all around.' He squatted by the mare's shoulder, trying to help her stand.

'How do you know?' Alison demanded. 'Why should we believe you and not Chance?'

On the rocky ledge above them, Chance Williams waited. He was cold and stiff from sitting in one position and trying not to make a sound. The blasted mustang stallion would be back, sometime during this night. There was nothing to do but wait.

On a higher outcropping, something else was

waiting. The old cougar had cubs waiting nearby for food. But she was starving and had no milk. The big cat had been watching the horse below, waiting for the foal to be born, but there were too many people, and a fire. The old cougar was almost blind, but she could see the flames and smell the smoke.

She could also smell the man crouched on the ledge below her.

This man was an easier target, and more sure. The cougar crept closer, on paws specially designed not to make the smallest sign. Her muscles bunched as she readied herself to spring.

Chance swung the rifle to his shoulder. There he was – the stallion, just coming into the firelight, come to fetch his mare. Twenty-five thousand dollars, on the hoof.

Chance closed one eye and looked down the telescopic sight. An easy shot! There was nothing to hunting mustangs – if you understood their ways.

*

'There he is!' Meg cried, as Wildfire stepped out of the shadows.

The stallion had fire in his eyes. He pawed the earth, shook his great head, furious at the scent of cat so close to Windy and her foal.

'Stay back,' Thomas warned. 'Don't get between the stallion and Windy. Don't make any sudden moves. He's still nervous about us, and wild.'

The three girls walked slowly backwards until they were standing beside Thomas on the other side of the fire, leaving space for Wildfire to come close to the mare.

He whickered urgently to Windy and she raised her head. Wildfire sniffed around the entire area, curling his upper lip to trap the molecules of the new foal's scent forever in his memory bank.

Then he nudged Windy with his nose. It was

just as if he were repeating Thomas's warning.
'Come on, get up, move, there is danger!'

Once more Windy responded to the stallion's
strength. She tried to get her forefeet out in front
of her, and then to rise. She staggered up,
breaking the umbilical cord that still connected
her to the foal.

Meg turned away quickly – there was blood!

'What do we need to do?' Becky whispered to
Thomas.

'Nothing,' Thomas said. 'This is natural. The
filly won't bleed. She's on her own now,
completely separate from her mother.'

Wildfire was still moving restlessly around the
clearing, shaking his head, his tail high and his
long mane nearly brushing his knees.

Windy had turned and was licking her foal's
muzzle. The little filly had been struggling to
stand, and the licking knocked her off balance.
Becky made a quick move forward, as if to help,
but Thomas held her back. 'This is what the foal

needs,' he insisted. 'She'll be all right. She'll be walking like a pro in half an hour.'

'Will Wildfire take them away?' Becky turned an anguished face to him.

'I don't know,' Thomas shook his head. 'It depends how much he trusts us. He's had some bad experiences with people.'

Chapter 12

SILENT HUNTER

Chance Williams slid back the oiled safety catch on his rifle very slowly. He knew the mustang's sharp hearing would catch any strange and unfamiliar sound. Damn, it was hard to get a clear shot with those kids and that interfering Indian in the way!

There! The position was perfect. Nothing but the horse in his gun sights. He squeezed the trigger.

Above him, the cougar had also timed her spring – waiting until she was in a perfect position. Her sudden leap spoiled Chance's aim, and the recoil of the rifle saved his life. The cougar struck him a glancing blow.

The bullet whined over Wildfire's head, missing the crest of his mane by a hair.

Down below, Meg heard the explosion of the gun, the whine as it hit the rock and Thomas's sudden cry as the bullet ricocheted back and threw him to the ground.

Up on the ledge the cougar whipped her lean body around for a second attack on Chance. But before she could launch herself through the air there was a scream of fury from below.

Wildfire mounted the ledge of rock in two great leaps, loose stones spinning out from under his powerful hooves.

The cat turned to meet this new danger.

It was a short and terrible struggle. With all the

pent-up power of his hatred for this silent hunter, Wildfire descended on the cougar with bared teeth and sharp, pounding hooves.

The cougar fought back, leaping for the jugular vein on the stallion's great, outstretched neck. She was not fighting for food now, but for her life, and the life of her cubs. Hunger had weakened her and Wildfire's fury was strong.

He reared and pounded at the cougar's body again and again. Finally, the cougar lay still.

In the clearing below, Meg knelt beside Thomas, her heart pounding with terror. 'He's been shot!' she screamed. 'Help me!' The sight of blood staining Thomas's upper arm made the world swim blackly in front of her eyes.

'I'm . . . all right,' Thomas grunted between clenched teeth. 'Chance still has the gun. Be careful!'

Meg threw him a backward glance of horror

and ran for the rocky outcropping. From the ledge above came the screams of a fierce battle. Meg scrambled up the rocks, following the route Wildfire had taken. She could see the stallion rear and plunge at the cougar.

Where was Chance?

Chance Williams had rolled away from the stallion and the cougar. Meg could see only his dark shape.

'I'm over here!' she heard his hoarse cry. 'The bloody cat mauled me – get me my gun!'

'The gun!' Meg shouted. 'Where is it?'

'There . . . by the edge. Hand it to me,' Chance cried. 'I'm going to shoot that beast if it's the last thing I do!'

Meg scrambled for the rifle. She picked it up and hurled it into the darkness as far as she could. 'You're not shooting anything!' she screamed at him.

For a moment she wanted to kick and stomp on the helpless man the way Wildfire had stomped on the cougar. She took a deep breath. There would be time to deal with Chance later. She must get back to Thomas.

Meg slipped and skidded down the steep rocky slope. Alison and Becky had propped Thomas up by the fire and Becky was tying a strip of his shirt firmly around his upper arm.

'Enough!' Thomas tried to grin. 'I need some circulation in that arm.' His face was pale and his upper lip damp with sweat. Meg ran to get a water bottle from her saddle bag.

Thomas drank gratefully and flexed his wrist. 'It's not serious,' he announced. 'Stop looking so tragic.'

'Maybe you should take some water up to Chance,' Meg told Alison. 'He was clawed by the cougar.'

'What happened up there?' Alison's dark eyes were huge.

'The cougar attacked Chance, but Wildfire saved his miserable hide,' Meg said. 'The cougar's dead.'

'Was Chance trying to shoot the cougar?'
Alison asked.

Meg was silent for a moment. When was
Alison going to get it? 'No,' she finally said. 'He
was shooting at Wildfire.'

Chapter 13

MEG TAKES CHARGE

'How do you know that?' Alison demanded, outraged.

'Let's go ask him,' Meg said, yanking Alison to her feet. 'Bring the water.' She had never dared boss Alison before, but someone had to get through her thick hide that Chance was no hero!

Becky climbed with them.

'Look who's here,' Chance turned on his side

and moaned. 'It's that pretty little filly, and her two friends. I knew you'd help me out.'

Meg's anger boiled over. How dare he!

'You're such a big brave cowboy, you don't need any help,' she shouted at him. 'Look what you've done, all by yourself!' She pointed down at the dead cougar. 'One dead mountain lion. One clawed cowboy – you! One guy with his arm shot up. One mare who almost died having her foal, and one foal who may not make it. All because you want your precious bounty money!'

'Who says I done all that?' Chance spat in the dirt. 'Give me some of that water.'

'You'll die of thirst and we'll leave you out here without your horse or your gun unless you tell the truth,' Meg said coldly. 'Did you let Windy out of her foaling box to act as bait to catch Wildfire?'

'Who says I did?' Chance reached for the water bottle.

Meg jerked it back.

'Meg –' Alison pleaded.

'Be quiet!' Meg said. 'Well? Did you sneak into the barn and open that foaling stall or didn't you?'

'All right, I did. What are you going to do about it? Give me some water.'

'How could you?' Becky said furiously.

Meg handed Chance the bottle without a word.

'OK, how about getting me my horse?' Chance said, after swallowing half the bottle.

'Those claw wounds on your neck are probably septic,' Meg said coldly. 'You need them cleaned up and bandaged, before you do any more riding.' Meg couldn't look closely at the damage the cougar had done, but her words seemed to scare Chance.

'So get me a bandage.' He winced. 'I don't need no infection.'

'Are you the bounty hunter or not?' Meg said. 'Tell the truth.'

'So, I'm the big bad wolf,' Chance grinned

unpleasantly at the three of them. 'I've been hunting that horse, and I'll keep on hunting him. What good is he alive? He'll just keep stealing mares, including yours,' he nodded at Becky, 'and turning them wild so they have to be retrained or they're good for nothin'. He's got to be shot, same as any other rogue animal.'

'I'm goin' back down to look after Windy and her foal.' Becky turned away.

Meg glanced at her. She could tell some of what Chance had said had hit home to Becky.

'Wildfire has a right to live,' Meg insisted. 'We'll work out another way besides shooting him.'

'I can't believe it,' Alison was shaking her head at Chance. 'I was so wrong about you. You're a bounty hunter. You kill animals for money!'

'Well, life is full of little disappointments,' Chance said. 'Now, how about my horse?'

'I don't think so,' Meg said firmly. 'We have more important things to think about besides looking after some greedy rogue animal! We'll see about your horse later. Let's go,' she said to Alison, leading the way back down to the fire.

'I can't believe it,' Alison was still muttering. 'He seemed like such a cool guy – I feel like such an idiot!'

Meg put an arm around her shoulders. 'Don't worry about it,' she said. 'I could have made the same mistake myself. Come on. Right now we need to get Windy and the foal safely back to the ranch.'

'I can carry the foal across my saddle.' Becky knelt down and cuddled the little filly in her arms. 'It's too far for her to walk.'

'How about you,' Meg turned to Thomas. 'Can you ride that far?'

'I can, but I'm not going in that direction.' Thomas shook his head. 'You didn't notice, but Wildfire has gone. He just melted away after the fight with the cougar. I have to go after him.'

'Thomas!' Meg shouted. 'You're wounded. You can't go riding off in the dark!'

'The mustang might be hurt, too,' Thomas
said quietly.

'That stupid horse again,' Becky shouted. 'It's
always that stupid horse!'

'I know he's caused you trouble.' Thomas's
brown eyes were full of sympathy. 'But for me
he represents a dream. I can see a whole herd of
great horses coming from Wildfire, horses like
that little filly in your arms. He's one of the last
great mustangs, and his line will be preserved – if
I can just catch him and convince him it's a good
idea.' Thomas winced and grabbed his wounded
arm.

'It's hurting a lot, isn't it?' Meg said. 'How are
you going to ride?'

'If one of you can help me fix up a sling to hold
my arm steady,' Thomas grunted, 'I'll be all right.'

'This is crazy!' Meg whipped off her sweatshirt
angrily and folded it into a rough triangle to
make a sling. 'If you're really going to ride after
Wildfire, then I'm going with you.'

'Then Becky and I will have to ride back to the ranch by ourselves!' Alison's voice rose. 'How will we find our way?'

Thomas was already standing by Palouse, ready to go. 'There's a short cut just on the other side of the ridge,' he told them. 'It's an old wagon road that leads to the main fork in the trail. When you get there take the right branch and it will lead you straight to the ranch.'

Becky was nodding. 'Do you think Windy can make it?' she asked.

'You're only about an hour's ride if you take that short cut,' Thomas told her. 'Go slow, stop often, and give Windy just a little water at a time.'

'But we can't see! It's so dark!' Alison was still complaining.

'The moon will soon be up,' Thomas told her. 'And horses have good night vision. They'll get you there.'

Meg had been shoving every spare water bottle and scrap of food in Brownie's saddle bag for their trek. 'What about Chance?' she said over her shoulder. 'Should we just leave him up there?'

'Yes!' Alison said furiously.

'No.' Thomas sighed reluctantly.

The four of them helped Chance down to the fire. Thomas led his horse off into the trees and tied it where it could graze. The girls lugged the saddle back to the fire for Chance to lean on.

'I've got some whiskey in my saddle bag somewhere. Leave me that,' Chance growled.

'Forget it,' Alison said. 'I'd like you to suffer for shooting at us.'

Meg suddenly remembered the gun. She hunted through the brush at the base of the rocky outcropping and came up with the rifle. 'We shouldn't leave this here . . .'

'My dad will want it,' Becky said grimly. 'He'll be back for you, don't worry,' she told Chance. 'He really hates people who shoot at wild animals.'

She climbed into Hank's saddle. Meg and Alison handed up the struggling bundle of legs that was Windy's foal. As soon as she felt herself safely draped over the saddle and close to Becky she stopped squirming.

'Good luck,' Meg said.

'I still can't believe you're going out after that mustang,' Alison whispered as she turned Sugar to mount him. 'Why don't you change your mind?'

'I'll be all right,' Meg promised. 'It's Thomas I'm worried about.'

'Take my advice,' Alison said bitterly. 'Never worry about guys!'

Chapter 14

RETURN TO THE RANCH

Becky stroked the little foal stretched across the saddle in front of her as they rode back towards the ranch. Every few minutes she would try to wriggle out of Becky's grip, tire herself with the struggle and rest quietly again. This was one of her quiet moments, and Becky took a long breath.

'You're going to be a great horse some day,'

she said. 'You'll be fast and strong like your
mother and able to run all day like your dad. I
think I'll call you Night Breeze – maybe Breezy
for your stable name. We'll have to see if it fits.'

Becky knew the little filly liked to listen to her
talk. Her ears, which seemed too big for her tiny
head, rotated to catch every word. She also
seemed to like the slow, up and down rhythm of
the horse underneath her. Becky stroked her
from her ears to her bottle-brush tail.

Never in her life had Becky felt this way about
a horse. From the moment of Breezy's birth a
bond had been formed between them. Breezy
had tottered after Becky and had to be convinced
that her mother Windy was the source of
nourishment and life.

Becky knew that this was called imprinting,
but the word didn't even start to describe how
you felt when a helpless little animal turned to
you for love and comfort. It was so important to
get her safely back to the ranch!

I can train her, Becky thought. I can look after her and teach her and she'll be my horse. The idea thrilled and scared her at the same time. This is how Meg must feel about Silver, she realised. No wonder she misses him.

The old wagon road was smooth, well-beaten sand, good footing for the horses.

'It's easier to ride at night than I thought,' Becky called to Alison, who was just a darker shape in the darkness beside her. 'I'm thinking of calling the filly Night Breeze – Breezy for short. Do you like it?'

'Sure,' Alison called back. She was glad of this time to ride alone in the dark and think about Chance. She didn't want to talk right now. Something inside of her felt bruised and angry. She needed to figure out why she had been so sure she was right about him. Why hadn't she realised he was a great big phony?

'The moon is rising,' Becky said. 'Just like Thomas said it would.'

A bright three-quarter moon looked like it had been flung into the sky above the highest mountain peak. The whole world seemed to shimmer and they could see the pale sand trail winding ahead of them.

'I hope Meg's brilliant friend Thomas is right about this old road leading to the ranch.' Alison peered down the moonlit path. 'There are so many trails up here – how could he be sure?'

'People who live up here in the back country like Thomas and my dad notice every trail and where it leads.' Becky shifted the weight of the foal in front of her. 'It's like you know the streets in the city.'

'Well, I know he's Mr Wonderful, but I'll feel a lot better when I can see the ranch,' Alison grumbled. It didn't help that Meg had been right about Thomas. What was she, some great expert on guys all of a sudden?

The foal had started wriggling on the saddle in front of Becky again. 'Time for a nutrition break,' she called, signalling Brownie to stop.

While Breezy, as they were now calling the foal was nursing, Becky and Alison finished the chocolate bars in their knapsacks.

'What are those lights down there?' Alison said a few moments later with her mouth full of candy. 'They look like they're moving!'

She yanked on Becky's sleeve. Becky was totally entranced watching Breezy – her legs splayed out, her brush of a tail waving back and forth like a happy flag – nursing as if she been doing this for days instead of hours.

Becky glanced in the direction Alison was pointing. Three lights were bobbing up and down. They disappeared for a moment and then appeared again.

'They must be looking for us!' Alison was jumping up and down in the moonlight. 'I wish we had a light so we could signal them.'

Becky scrabbled through her saddle bags. 'Flashlights – the one thing we forgot!'

'Look! They're heading in the wrong direction!' Alison pointed at the lights which were swinging off to the right. 'We have to do something – yell, scream, anything!'

'They're too far away to hear us screamin',' Becky said, 'but I've got Chance's gun.'

They had taken the gun as important evidence that Chance had been shooting at Wildfire. The rifle was wrapped in a raincoat and tied on the back of Alison's saddle.

'Do you know how to fire it?' Alison asked, as she untied the leather thongs that held the long thin bundle and handed it to Becky. 'I'd be scared.'

'It's not hard.' Becky unwrapped the gun. 'The only thing is, it might terrify Windy and the foal. I don't want them to be frightened of loud noises.'

'I'll stand by Windy's head and reassure her,' Alison said. 'I don't think Breezy cares about anything except getting her tummy as full as possible!'

'All right.' Becky took a few steps away from the horses, released the safety catch, pointed the gun at the sky and fired. 'That should bring them runnin',' she grinned, as the sound echoed back from a hundred peaks.

Chapter 15

MOONLIGHT RIDE

Meg had never ridden by moonlight before.
The trees, the bunchgrass, the peaks of the
mountains above them were all bathed in the
same silvery glow. It was like riding in a dream,
Meg thought, and only the clop of Brownie's
feet and the steady sound of his breathing was
like everyday reality.

At first she was frightened. 'I can't see

where to go,' she told Thomas.

'Your horse can see,' Thomas reassured her. 'Just trust him.'

So Meg rode along on sturdy old Brownie, following the shimmering moonlight path across the valley. She wondered where this night's adventure would lead. Thomas was tracking Wildfire, following the barest traces of his passage.

At last he pointed to the foot of a sloping alpine meadow. 'Up there,' he said in a low voice. 'Can you see him?'

Meg shook her head. 'It's too dark!'

'Watch for movement – look! There he goes, to the left of those trees.'

Meg peered ahead where Thomas pointed. She thought she could make out a darker shape, running along the top of the meadow. 'I think I see something . . . maybe.'

Suddenly Thomas gave a sharp gasp.

When she turned to him he was holding his

wounded arm, and his face was ghastly white in the moonlight. 'What's the matter?' Meg asked urgently.

'I'm . . . all right,' Thomas said between gritted teeth. At the same moment he slowly slid from Palouse's back and collapsed on the dew-soaked grass.

Meg threw herself off Brownie. Her fingers fumbled with the buckle on her saddle bag as she reached for the water bottle to take to Thomas.

'You can't ride all night chasing a wild horse,' she said, watching his hand shake as he brought the bottle to his lips. 'You're too weak. Let's go back and get help!'

'You're right, I can't do the riding we have to do tonight,' Thomas tried to grin as he wiped the top of the water bottle and handed it back. 'It's a good thing you're here to do it for me.'

'Me!' Meg couldn't believe her ears. 'What are you talking about?'

'You can take Palouse. He knows what he's

doing,' Thomas said. 'I wouldn't ask you to go after Wildfire by yourself if I didn't know you'd be safe.'

'Thomas, what are you saying?' Meg tried to keep the tremble out of her voice.

'I'm saying that Wildfire is tired, confused and maybe badly chewed up by the cougar. He's also alone. He knows we're behind him, making him run when all he'd really like to do is hole up somewhere and get his strength back.'

'So, why don't we leave him alone?'

'Because he isn't safe, for one thing,' Thomas said. 'Chance didn't get him, but maybe the next bounty hunter will. And for another thing, he doesn't really want to be alone. Horses are herd animals, they need other horses, especially when they're vulnerable, like Wildfire is right now. If you ride after him until he's really tired – don't crowd him, just keep him moving – and then stop, and ride slowly back away from him, I'm betting he'll follow you, back to me.'

'Meanwhile, you're just going to lie here, by yourself? Thomas Horne, I think you've got brain fever. This is dangerous and dumb!' Meg was terrified of what he was asking her to do.

'I won't be alone, I've got Brownie,' Thomas said. 'Saddle up Palouse now and get going, or you'll lose the mustang.'

Meg could see there was no use arguing with Thomas. She tossed him the rain gear from the back of her saddle – it would at least keep him off the damp ground. She took off Brownie's saddle and saddled Palouse who pranced and bobbed his head as if eager to go.

'Don't worry if you lose sight of the stallion,' Thomas said. 'Palouse will know where he is.'

Meg would not forget that ride for the rest of her life. Across high mountain meadows, down steep slopes and through stands of trees, Palouse followed Wildfire at a slow, steady pace, stopping to rest when Wildfire stopped, moving on when the mustang moved again.

As the moon rose higher in the night sky, the light grew brighter. Meg could see her shadow, on Palouse, pacing along beside them. She could almost see the green of the grass at their feet.

At last, when Wildfire stopped to drink in a shallow river, Palouse drank too, further downstream. The moonlight made a shining pathway between the two horses. Meg decided it was now or never.

She slowly turned Palouse, leaned forward and whispered in his ear, 'Find Thomas, but don't go too fast.'

She held her breath as Palouse splashed up out of the stream and headed back the way they had come. Would the slender moonlight tie between the two horses hold? she wondered. Would the wild horse decide to come with them or make a dash for freedom?

She heard splashing, upstream, but did not

dare look back. 'Be relaxed,' Thomas had said. 'Don't act excited or too eager.' Meg prayed he was right and that Wildfire was there in the shadows behind them.

She tried to relax in the saddle. Once you got used to riding in the dark, it wasn't really too hard. She was so tired that the gentle rhythm of Palouse's movement almost put her to sleep. A couple of times she thought she dozed off, and even dreamed a little – of Thomas, waiting somewhere ahead of them, of Silver, pacing his stall at home. Silver could never have managed this rough terrain, but she wished he were walking beside her – how fantastic he'd look in the moonlight with his almost pure white hide and silvery mane.

Meg's head bobbed forward. She thought of Alison and for the first time in her life she felt sorry for her. Alison must be feeling betrayed and sad at the same time. It wasn't really Alison's fault that she fell for every good-looking guy that crossed her path. She was just built with a boy radar that never switched off.

Thinking of Alison made her furious with Chance all over again. She could see his sarcastic, sneering face. How dare he talk to her that way – as if she could ever be interested in a man like that!

And that brought her full turn to Thomas. What if Thomas had turned out to be the bounty hunter, instead of Chance? No, it was impossible, Meg decided. From the first instant she'd seen him she knew he was good and gentle and that she could trust him. He was like his horse, with a strong loyal heart that would never let you down.

Meg's head drooped forward and her eyes closed. She was jolted awake by Palouse stepping over a fallen tree in his path. He was an amazing horse! His feet never slipped into a gopher hole or tripped over a fallen tree. He knew exactly where he was going.

What a pampered, uninteresting life Silver and

the other stable horses led compared to this. Thomas had taught her how intelligent horses were, how their herd instincts were so sharp and fine, their sense of smell and direction so keen that they could find their herd over vast distances.

At last, Meg sensed that morning was coming. The moon was setting over the mountains behind her and a slight dawn breeze ruffled her hair. Meg had been up all night before, at sleepovers. But this wasn't like staying up at a friend's house where you ate and watched videos. This night felt like a week! It seemed ages since they had found Windy in the bog the evening before!

As the first grey light of morning broke, Meg looked back. There was Wildfire, his head down, patiently following, just as Thomas said he would. Meg felt a warm glow spread through her chilled body. She'd done it! She'd brought a wild mustang stallion back.

Palouse blew softly and swished his tail as if to let her know they were close to their goal. As the darkness thinned Meg saw Thomas stretched out on her yellow rain gear just ahead. Her heart bounded with anxiety – she had been gone hours – was he still all right?

Thomas winced as he sat up and smiled at Meg. 'I see you've brought in our friend.'

'Wildfire followed us, just like you said he would,' she said softly. 'How are you?'

'I'm a little stiff and sore,' Thomas said. 'Any more water?'

'Sure.' Meg got off Palouse and brought Thomas a full water bottle from the saddle bag.

'Now what?' she asked as Thomas gratefully gulped it down.

'Now is the hardest part,' Thomas sighed. 'We have to get him to trust us enough to get a rope on him and let us lead him back to the ranch.'

'How can we do that?' Meg rubbed her tired forehead.

'I've done it many times. I get up close to him, on foot, talk to him, win his trust.'

'Isn't it dangerous? You said to stay away from Wildfire, back at the rock when Windy's foal was born.'

Thomas smiled at her. 'The only time it's dangerous is when he feels cornered. Out here, where he has lots of space to run if he wants, it's very safe. You'll see – help me up.'

He took her hand, and Meg felt the thrill run all the way up her arm.

Chapter 16

WILDFIRE RUNS

'I'd like to have all day to get Wildfire used to us,' Thomas said. 'But we're going to have to do it in a couple of hours. My arm is not doing so well.' He sagged back to the ground.

Meg glanced at his bloody sleeve, and looked away quickly. As the light increased she saw Thomas's face was the colour of stove ashes, grey and chalky. His brown eyes were narrowed and dull with pain and she could see that every movement cost him great effort.

'Let me feel your forehead,' Meg ordered.

Thomas leaned close.

Meg reached out and placed a cool hand above his eyes. His skin was surprisingly soft, but burning hot. She longed to stroke his hair and touch the lines beside his mouth.

'You have a fever!' Meg gulped.

'Don't take your hand away,' Thomas said with a sigh. 'I think you have the healing touch. No wonder the horses like you . . .'

Meg let herself smooth back his straight black hair. 'You can't get close to Wildfire when you're on fire yourself with fever,' she told him. 'Tell me what to do. I'll try, if you promise to lie still and save your strength.'

'Wildfire's not going to like the rope,' Thomas said. 'He's had terrible experiences with men trying to rope him. You'll have to get him used to your touch first. Get him to come to you.'

He squeezed Meg's hand. 'I know you can do it,' he told her. He hesitated, but didn't let go of her hand. 'Look, this isn't a good time to say it, with the two of us out here alone, and everything, but you look so beautiful right now. I think you're – wonderful.'

'You're delirious,' Meg said.

'I know . . . I shouldn't say anything. You're too young. How old are you?'

'Fourteen,' Meg whispered. 'How old are you?'

'Seventeen.'

They stared at each other. 'Much too young!' they both said together, and then laughed, because they'd both said the same thing at the same time.

Thomas let go of Meg's hand. She jumped to her feet. At that moment, Meg would have gone through fire or jumped off a cliff for Thomas. Her heart was thumping. She turned to look for Wildfire, filled with a wild determination.

Wildfire was grazing a short distance away. The

sun came over a jagged peak above them and threw a beam of light on his reddish coat. He tossed his head, as if throwing off the sunbeam impatiently.

As she swished towards him through the wet grass, Meg could see the damage the cougar had done. Under Wildfire's throat, the skin was torn and the wound had clotted with blood and dirt.

'We'll clean that up and you'll feel better.' Meg took a few more cautious steps towards him. She kept her voice low and steady.

At the sound of her voice, Wildfire jerked up his head and eyed her curiously.

'He's going to run,' Thomas called softly. 'Approach him on Palouse. That's how he's used to seeing you and he knows Palouse is no threat to him.'

Meg turned slowly, careful not to make any quick movements he might see as threatening. In one smooth motion, she mounted Palouse, then rode close to Wildfire and let him sniff and see the horse and rider he'd been following all night.

'Yes, we're your friends,' Meg told him. When Palouse got close enough, she reached over and gently stroked Wildfire's shoulder. He jerked away at first, and then came to accept Meg's touch.

'That's good,' Thomas called. 'Now see if you can get him to let you touch him when you're on the ground, not on Palouse.'

Meg slipped from Palouse's back and stood very still, letting Wildfire get used to her on two legs. Then she reached out her hand and let him sniff it. Gently, very softly, she stroked the bridge of his nose.

It reminded her of touching Thomas. The thrill of communication was so strong it brought tears to Meg's eyes. It was as if she could see into Wildfire's mind. This wild creature wanted to trust her.

She reached up to stroke Wildfire on his neck,

ran her fingers through his tangled mane, patted his shoulders and chest. She was careful not to touch him near his wounds. If he seemed nervous she backed off, then tried again,

'There's one more thing,' Thomas called. 'It's an Aboriginal horse trainer's trick my grandfather taught me. You blow your breath softly into his nostrils so he will be sure of your scent.'

Meg stared at him. Breathe into the nostrils of a wild horse! Was he joking? 'Shouldn't you do this part?' she asked. 'He's going to be your horse.'

Thomas shook his head. 'You're the one who is making the first connection Wildfire's ever had with a human being. It has to be you.'

'Thomas . . .' Meg said. 'Are you sure?'

'I'm not sure why it works, but I've seen my grandfather do it many times.'

But first you have to get the horse to stand still, Meg thought. And you have to be close to those big teeth and flashing front hooves if he rears. She had a sudden image of Wildfire stomping and pounding the cougar. She brushed that picture out of her mind.

She came close to Wildfire's left side again. 'Here is where I have to trust you,' she told the great, proud horse. 'I have to tame you by sharing my breath with you. I hope you've heard of this old horse gentler's method.'

Meg stood close to Wildfire, stroking his long mane, trying to see the world as he saw it. She realised this is what she'd been doing with horses for a long time. She'd been able to visualise what Silver was thinking, when he was a frightened colt. She'd been linked to Windy when she was in the bog and when her foal was being born. Now she had to make the same link to Wildfire.

She moved a little so she was partly facing Wildfire, cupped his chin in her hand, leaned forward and gently blew into his wide nostrils.

Wildfire stood still. Meg blew again, and Wildfire snorted as if to say 'That's enough.'

'Good,' Meg heard Thomas call softly. 'Now the rope. Get it from Palouse's saddle and let the mustang smell it and get used to it. Take your time.'

Meg backed slowly away, talking constantly to Wildfire. 'This next part is easy,' she told him. 'We're going to teach you to walk with a lead rope so we can take you back to Mustang Mountain Ranch. Windy is there, and your foal, and you'll be safe.'

Meanwhile she had reached for the coiled rope and held it out to Wildfire. He backed away at the first sight of it.

His head and tail went up, and the proud, dangerous look was back in his eye. He pawed the ground, wheeled, and ran.

'Thomas, I've lost him,' Meg groaned. 'He's gone!'

Chapter 17

THE
GENTLE WAY

'Just stand still and quiet,' Thomas told her. 'And hope he comes back.'

Wildfire galloped, tail high, a glorious sight in the morning sun. For a moment Meg was sure he would disappear over the ridge. But at the top he stopped and half-turned to look curiously at her. She saw him etched against the sky, gazing down, choosing, in the full power of his freedom, whether to come back.

She couldn't swallow, could hardly breathe. The rope still in her hand, she turned so her body was sideways to the horses. Her arms were loose at her side, her head a little drooped. 'We won't hurt you,' she repeated over and over again. 'You're safe with us.'

At last, out of the corner of her eye, she saw the quick flash of motion as Wildfire turned and walked down the slope towards her. He stopped just a few paces away, snorted, moved forward and flared his nostrils at Meg as if to say, 'OK, what's next?'

'What should I do now?' she called to Thomas.

'This is a very good sign,' Thomas told her. 'He's signalling he wants to join up with us. It might be because you have the scent of Windy and her foal on your clothes. The old-time mustangers, my grandfather says, never changed their clothes when they were trying to catch a wild horse. They knew the horse would get comfortable with their scent.'

Meg offered Wildfire the rope for another sniff. Once again he jerked his head back, but this time he didn't run. Meg glanced over at Thomas, sitting cross-legged, watching the stallion.

'We have a problem,' Thomas said. 'We can't use a rope on him. I didn't realise the cougar had clawed his neck so bad.'

'What should we do?' Meg knew Thomas was right. A rope, rubbing on those raw wounds, would panic Wildfire.

'We'll have to ride back to the ranch and hope he follows us all the way.' Thomas rose stiffly to his feet. Clutching his wounded arm, he took an unsteady step forward and almost fell.

Meg rushed forward to support him. 'How are you going to ride when you can hardly stand?'

Thomas grinned at her, a lopsided grin because he was hurting. 'You're going to have to help me up on Palouse's back,' he said, 'and tie me to the saddle.'

She could feel the fever burning through Thomas's shirt. 'I'll ride behind you and hold you on,' she said. 'Brownie will follow without being tied, I'm sure.'

Meg led Palouse closer. She let Thomas stand on her bended knee to heave himself into the saddle while Palouse cooperated by standing still. Thomas held the reins in his good hand so Meg could scramble up behind him.

It felt so strange to be pressed against his body. Meg felt him shiver as she put her arms around his waist. She smelled his unfamiliar smell and felt his rough braid against her cheek.

'Ready?' Thomas grinned at her over his shoulder and urged Palouse forward. 'Let's go, friend horse. Get us all back to Mustang Mountain Ranch.'

Half an hour later a slow procession wound its way down towards the Mustang Mountain

Ranch. Palouse, then Brownie, and a good distance behind, Wildfire. Thomas barely managed to stay upright in the saddle, even with Meg's help.

Palouse seemed to understand that he should move slowly and Meg was glad. Part of her wished this ride would never end. She loved being so close to Thomas, without looking at him, without feeling awkward and shy. Another part of her was desperate to get him to help and safety.

She held on to him tightly, sending Thomas her strength, telling him about Silver to keep him awake. 'Silver's not really my horse,' she said. 'I know that someday he'll have to go back to his home stable in Maryland for more training. But I love him so much, I don't think about him leaving.' I feel the same about you, she longed to say.

She glanced back to make sure Wildfire was still following. His ears were swivelled forward to catch Meg's voice. 'As for you,' she told the mustang, 'you're going to have a great life with Thomas and his grandfather – your own herd of mares and foals, lots of good grazing, shelter and food when the winter storms bury the grass too deep, a place where you'll be king.'

Half an hour later they reached a part of the mountainside where dead black trees stuck up like pointed fingers. 'I know where we are,' Meg gasped. 'This is where the forest fire burned last summer. Just over the next rise we'll be able to see the ranch. What will Wildfire do when he sees the fences and the buildings?'

Thomas stirred in the saddle and lifted his head. 'He'll be wary. He'll know Windy is down there, but the fences will make him nervous. I wish we had some outriders to help herd him in.'

'Stop,' Meg said. 'I've got an idea.'

Chapter 18

CORRAL

'Look, Mom, isn't she beautiful?' Becky's face was shining as she looked up at her mother. She was on her knees in the large sunlit corral, hugging Breezy around the neck, her face pressed into the foal's sweet-smelling mane.

Laurie felt tears come to her eyes. 'It's a beautiful sight,' she agreed. Never had Becky looked this excited about anything, let alone a horse! Her daughter had changed in her year away at school, Laurie thought. Going away had been good for Becky. She seemed more at peace with herself, less angry at everyone and everything.

'Think about it, Mom! She'll have Wildfire's endurance and Windy's speed. She'll be such a great horse –' Becky suddenly stood up.

'Mom, there's a horse coming.'

Laurie shaded her eyes. A lone horse was loping down the long slope towards the ranch.

'It looks like Brownie, and Meg, riding bareback with just a halter rope!' Becky said, astonished.

Becky opened the gate of the big corral. Meg rode in on Brownie. 'We need help to herd Wildfire into the corral,' she panted, slipping off his back. 'He's followed us most of the way, but Thomas doesn't think he'll come in by himself.'

'We don't want Wildfire here!' Becky cried. 'What if he goes after Windy and her foal?'

'You look exhausted.' Laurie Sandersen put her hand on Meg's shoulder. 'Come and rest.'

'NO!' Meg shook her head like an angry horse. 'Don't you understand? We've spent the whole night trying to get Wildfire back to this ranch. Thomas is really sick, and he's risked his life and if you won't help I'll go back to him and we'll try to coax Wildfire in by ourselves. Just, please, leave the gate open?'

She threw herself back up on Brownie's broad back.

'Meg, wait. You can't go riding off like this,' Becky begged.

'At least get a saddle and bridle on that horse,' Laurie insisted.

'No time,' Meg shook her head again. 'I don't even know if Thomas will still be conscious when I get back.'

She rode out of the corral, leaving Becky and her mother staring after her.

Chapter 19

FENCES IN SIGHT

Thomas was conscious when Meg reached him, but just barely. He was slumped along Palouse's neck, his hair blending with the horse's mane and his good arm dragging.

'Thomas!' Meg called softly. She could see Wildfire, not far away, grazing on the mountain meadow grass.

Thomas lifted his head slowly and gazed at her

with glassy eyes. 'You're back?' He seemed surprised. 'I thought you'd gone.'

'Don't you remember? I went to get help.' But Thomas fell forward again, weak with fever.

Meg swung up on the saddle behind him. He was burning hot, and his shirt was damp with sweat. 'Come on,' she said gently. 'We're going to take Wildfire down to the ranch.'

She crossed her fingers that Becky and her mother had put Windy and her baby safely in the barn and left the gate open for them. She wouldn't tell Thomas that they didn't want Wildfire. She'd just concentrate on getting Thomas safely to Mustang Mountain Ranch. He needed help!

She clucked to Palouse to go forward and checked to see if Wildfire noticed they were moving. He lifted his head, snorted and started after them, as if on an invisible rope. Good, but the real test would come when the ranch was in sight. Would he follow them down into captivity or run for it when he saw the fences?

She held her breath as they came over the rise and started down the long slope towards the ranch. Halfway down she glanced back and the mustang was still following. Then, from out of nowhere, two riders appeared above them and on either side. She recognised Slim and another ranch hand, waving their hats and hollering and herding Wildfire towards the open gate. Below, she could see that the corral gate was open, and she urged Palouse into a jog, holding tight to Thomas so he wouldn't slide off. Meg felt a great spurt of happiness. Becky and her mom had decided to help, after all. They were her real, true friends.

Meg threw her arms around Becky. 'Thank you,' she whispered, pressing her face into the tangle of her friend's hair. Wildfire was in the corral. Thomas was standing by Palouse, holding on to his horse's neck for support, and grinning through his pain.

'Don't thank me,' Becky shrugged. 'It was my mother who convinced everybody to ride out and help bring in that big old mustang. Look at him! You'd think he owned the place.'

Wildfire was pacing around the large corral, turning this way and that, tossing his proud mane and looking puzzled, whinnying for Windy. She and her foal were shut safely in the barn.

'He'll be fine now,' Thomas said. He had loosened the cinch on the saddle and now slipped it from Palouse's back. The weight made his knees buckle and a spasm of pain crossed his face.

Meg could read him as clearly as the horse. Thomas was holding himself together by sheer will power. 'Here, let me take that,' Meg grabbed the saddle from Thomas and heard his sharp intake of breath.

'Becky,' Meg whispered urgently. 'Thomas's gunshot wound has made him feverish. Can we find a place for him to lie down?'

Laurie Sandersen hurried up, glanced at Thomas's ashen face and bloody arm and took charge. 'What have you two been up to? Never mind, I'll get the story later, but right now, young man, you need some doctoring!'

She bustled him away towards the ranch house.

'What about Chance?' Meg asked.

'My dad and a couple of hands are out lookin' for that skunk,' Becky sighed. 'They left right after Alison and I got back.'

Once Thomas was being well looked after, Meg went searching for Alison.

She found her in the bunkhouse. For once Alison wasn't the confident bouncy person who always had herself under firm control. There were spots of colour on her pale cheeks, and her smooth dark hair was rumpled.

They stared at each other, Alison on her bunk, Meg in the doorway.

'Come in and shut that door!' Alison ordered. 'Do you think I want the whole world to see me this way?'

Meg was relieved that Alison still sounded like herself.

'I suppose you're going to gloat, and tell me I told you so and say that anyone could have seen through that big phony, Chance,' Alison said with a catch in her voice.

'No,' Meg shook her head wearily. 'I could have made the same mistake with Thomas. I'm lucky he turned out to be nice.'

'You mean you like him?' Alison's dark eyes filled with tears. 'That's awful. It means it's all true!'

'What's all true?' Meg sat on Alison's bunk. She reached for Alison's hand, but Alison snatched hers away as if it had been burnt.

'It's all true that you're getting so cool, and guys like you and you like them back, and you're going to be taller than I am, and much better looking . . . oh, I can't stand it!' Alison threw herself face down and thumped desperately on her pillow.

'I was wrong,' Meg said. 'You haven't changed at all. Just tell me one thing, Alison. Why did you invite me here for the summer last year and this year – why did you want me here?'

'Because . . .' Alison sat up and stared at her. 'Because I needed you. You were never going to be competition.'

'That's why you chose me as a friend in the first place, isn't it?' Meg asked. 'Because I was always going to be lumpy, plain old Meg, and beside me you'd always look good.'

'But you're not lumpy and plain any more . . .' Alison wailed.

Meg got up and opened the bathroom door. She looked at herself in the full-length mirror.

A complete stranger looked back, tall, with a long neck and high cheekbones under the dirty tired face. A wide mouth and wide eyes. Long arms and long legs. Smooth brown hair in a tail that hung down her back. 'Thomas is right,' she laughed. 'I do look a bit like a horse.'

'No you don't,' Alison sobbed.

'I think he meant it as a compliment.' Meg grinned at her reflection. She shut the bathroom door and walked back to Alison's bunk. 'Anyway, I don't care what I look like. I just tamed a wild horse with my bare hands, and rode bareback all the way back to the ranch.'

She sat down wearily on her bunk, and gazed at Alison. 'I liked being your friend because you were perfect,' she told her. 'I figured that if you liked me, I couldn't be completely hopeless. But it looks like we're going to have to find another reason to be friends. I found out you're not perfect, and you found out I'm not hopeless.'

'I'm hopeless,' Alison wailed.

'No, you're not!' Meg insisted. 'Alison, out there in the clearing, you were a different person. You were terrific. You helped Windy have her foal, you even sacrificed your favourite sweatshirt. You didn't think about yourself and you were strong. Meanwhile, I was sitting there, trying not to throw up! You were terrific and that's the friend I want – the real you. Can't we forget all this stuff about looks?'

'I don't know,' Alison snuffled. 'Looks are very important to me.'

'Well, we'll talk about it tomorrow.' Meg lurched to her feet, took one step and collapsed on her own bunk. She pulled her pillow over her head. 'Now, I'm going to sleep.'

Chapter 20

A NEW TRAIL

The next morning, Alison was lying flat on her back staring at the wooden ceiling of the bunkhouse when Meg got up.

'I'm a complete loser,' Alison said tragically. 'I can see how totally selfish and self-centred I've been. I wouldn't blame you if you went home.'

'We'll see,' Meg sighed. Alison had changed in some ways and not in others, she decided.

Becky had left her a clean set of clothes, neatly piled on the end of the bed, and a note:

'Gone to see Windy and the foal – see you at breakfast. Love, B.'

Meg dressed quickly, washed her face, brushed her teeth and pulled back her hair. She left without throwing Alison another glance. If she wanted to suffer dramatically – let her!

Meg found Thomas sitting in Dan Sandersen's office chair, with Laurie changing the dressing on his wound. 'This boy heals like lightning,' Laurie smiled. 'A good night's sleep and his fever is gone. The bullet just creased his skin, it's not too deep.'

Meg was glad when a fresh bandage covered the damage to Thomas's arm. She felt like the wound was to her own skin.

'There's one thing worrying me,' Thomas said. 'Those cougar cubs we left out there with no mother. They must be very young – she was still nursing them. They'll starve if we don't find them.'

'Your worries are over!' Dan Sandersen's lanky form appeared in the office door. 'When we found Chance last night he was complaining that some babies bawling kept him awake. When we went back this morning we found the den, and two kits, howling their heads off.'

'What are you going to do?' Laurie looked up from her bandaging. 'Take them to Mary's?'

'Yep.' Dan sat in his big cowhide armchair and stretched out his long legs. 'We've got a friend who has a refuge for wild animals that can't survive on their own,' Dan explained to Thomas and Meg. 'When they're old enough, Mary will release them to the wild.'

They all went out to inspect the cougar kittens in a roomy cage on the veranda.

'They're adorable!' Meg knelt down to pet them. The kits had white underbellies and ringed tails, otherwise they looked like any other fuzzy kittens.

'They'll have to be bottle-fed for awhile,'

Laurie said. 'Can you take it on, Meg?'

Meg nodded. 'I'll get Alison to help,' she said. It would give Alison something to think about besides her wasted life.

'It seems only fitting that their crying kept Chance awake all night,' Thomas laughed.

'What will happen to Chance now?' Meg asked.

Dan Sandersen's face clouded over. 'He's as hard to catch as a bad smell,' he told them. 'We'll nail him for a big fine for shooting animals in a wildlife preserve, but with those claw marks on him, he can always claim he was shooting at the lion in self-defence, not at Wildfire. I'm afraid that before it's all sorted out Chance Williams will be long gone.'

'As long as he stays away,' Laurie shuddered. 'To think I asked that man to breakfast!'

'How long will you stay?' Dan turned to Thomas.

Meg held her breath. The idea of Thomas leaving was so painful she hadn't allowed herself to think about it.

Thomas flapped his arm in its sling. 'Mrs Sandersen has fixed me up pretty well,' he said. 'We should be able to leave almost any time. I'm anxious to get Wildfire home and I think your wife and daughter can't wait till we go.'

'It's not your fault, Thomas,' Laurie Sandersen said apologetically. 'But Wildfire keeps pacing around the corral, threatening to kick the fence down to get to Windy and her foal. We can't get them to settle down while he's around, and they both need to rest.'

Dan Sandersen nodded. He looked from Thomas to Meg and back to Laurie. 'Then it seems to me there's only one thing to do,' he said. 'A couple of the hands and I will ride up to Rocky Mountain House with Thomas and the mustang. We'll make sure they don't run into any trouble, or any more bounty hunters like Chance.'

'You don't have to –' Thomas began.

'Of course I don't, but I've been wanting to see that country for a long time,' Dan said. 'There's a whole network of north–south trails between here and your land – it should take us about a week.'

He grinned at Thomas who was looking hard and proud and like he would insist on saying no.

'Don't swell up like a mustang stallion.' Dan shifted in his chair. 'I understand you want to make the trip yourself. But I figure you saved my wife's horse and her foal, and you got my girls home safe, and I owe you.'

'Could we go too?' Meg shot in before she knew the words were coming out of her mouth. 'I mean Alison and I and Becky if she wants to? I'd love to go on a really long trail ride through the back country, and Thomas, I did ride all night after Wildfire and I'd like to see where he's going to end up. I made all those promises to him about good grass, and his own herd, and lots of space.'

'I think it's a terrific idea,' Laurie said. 'I think I'll come too. It's about time I got back in the saddle and stopped babying myself.'

Chapter 21

THOMAS SAYS GOODBYE

A week later, Thomas and Wildfire were settled at his grandfather's ranch near Rocky Mountain House and the Mustang Mountain crew was ready to leave for the ride home.

Meg, her heart aching, went to look for Thomas and say goodbye.

Thomas was in a small sturdy round pen he and his grandfather had built, working with Wildfire.

Meg stood on the outside of the pen and watched.

Thomas had finished a long grooming session, and Wildfire's red coat gleamed as it never had before.

Thomas reached in his belt for a knife and cut off a long hank of his straight black hair. He began to braid it into Wildfire's mane.

Meg swallowed the lump in her throat. Why did everything Thomas do make her heart ache like this? It was such a simple thing, twisting your hair together, but somehow it meant that you and your horse were linked. No fancy ribbons, no decoration, just a simple joining of two locks of hair.

Thomas spoke without even turning to look at her. 'You can do this with Silver's mane when you get home,' he said. 'Maybe eagle feathers would be a bit extreme where you come from, but nobody would even notice a bit of your lovely hair mixed with his.'

'This week has been so great.' Meg tried to make her voice sound normal. 'I've learned so much from you – I wish you could teach me more.'

Thomas left Wildfire and came over to the fence. They stood close together, with the rails in between.

'Thank you for helping me get Wildfire, and for bringing him home,' Thomas said. He smiled down at her, turning her knees to water.

'Do you think Wildfire will stay here?' Meg asked. 'Do you think he'll forget Mustang Mountain?'

'I hope he will.' Thomas reached through the bars for Meg's hand. 'But I won't forget.'

Meg's heart thumped so loud she was sure Thomas could hear it. 'Remember when Windy pulled herself out of the bog and wanted to run with Wildfire?' she asked him.

Thomas nodded, his brown eyes serious.

'I made a promise to Windy that night,' Meg

said. 'I promised her she would run with him and be part of his herd some day. I guess that's a promise I'm not going to be able to keep. Becky and her mom are so anxious to train Windy and her foal as endurance horses. They'd never sell her or anything.' She bit her lip, and looked around the rim of mountains above them, trying not to cry.

'You don't know what the future will bring,' Thomas said gently. 'I'll keep in touch with the Sandersens, and I won't forget your promise. Maybe things will change and it will happen some day.'

He dropped her hand. 'And speaking of keeping in touch, I need your e-mail address,' he went on. 'You can ask me any training questions about Silver and I'll try to answer.'

Meg's face lit up. 'That will be great. We can stay in touch, and . . .'

'And hope that the four winds blow us together again.' Thomas smiled.

Step into the wild again as more drama and
danger await in the next Mustang Mountain
book . . .

Wild Horse

Here's a taste . . .

Chapter 1

BATTLES

The sleek black sports car pulled up outside the Blue Barn Stables. The doors opened and four people got out – two of them very squished from riding in the back seat.

Alison Chant and her mother paid no attention to the sadly rumpled pair who wriggled out behind them. They were too busy fighting.

Both were tall and dark, both had straight

backs and straight noses. Both were furious. Alison wore riding clothes, slim boots, close-fitting pants, a trim riding jacket. An expensive black riding helmet swung from her hand. Her mother, Marion, was dressed in a neat, well-fitted black suit. They could almost have been sisters, except there was a sag to Alison's young shoulders that didn't match her mother's stiff posture.

'You didn't prepare for the district finals properly, and you know it!' Marion Chant's tone was frigid.

'Oh, well as far as you're concerned, nothing is good enough. It wouldn't matter if I was out here riding twenty-four hours a day, it still wouldn't be enough.'

Becky Sandersen, Alison's cousin, and their friend Meg O'Donnell, exchanged embarrassed glances. 'C'mon,' Becky whispered, 'let's just go in.'

They gave a backwards, sympathetic glance

at Alison, as they headed for the stable door at Blue Barns.

'Sometimes I feel almost sorry for Alison.' Becky shook her honey-blonde curls. 'My Aunt Marion can be harsh.'

Becky and Alison were first cousins, and both were fourteen, but it would be hard to imagine two girls more different. Becky had grown up on ranches in the Rocky Mountains. She was lean and strong from fresh air and living outdoors. Her hair was blonde, instead of dark and her brown eyes seemed flecked with sunlight.

'I wish my aunt would just let up on Alison about the dressage competitions,' Becky sighed, as she and Meg headed for the tack room. 'Aunt Marion takes everything so seriously. Since I got here, two months ago, I don't think I've ever really heard her laugh. She hardly even smiles, just walks around with that sarcastic smirk on her face.'

Meg nodded. 'She's totally different from your

mom.' Meg had come to love Becky's mom, Laurie Sandersen, when she and Alison visited Becky's home in the Alberta Rockies. 'You must miss her.'

Becky gave a quick glance at the tall girl with the wide blue eyes that missed nothing. How typical of Meg to realise how homesick she was feeling. In fact, life with her aunt and uncle here in this suburb of New York would be next to unbearable without Meg. 'I even miss Mustang Mountain Ranch,' she said with a shaky laugh. 'Who would have thought I'd ever say that?'

When her parents had moved to the isolated Rocky Mountain ranch, Becky had thought her life had ended. Being thirteen in a place with no friends, towns, not even roads or a school was like a sentence. Then Alison and Meg had arrived, suddenly and unexpectedly. Over the past two summers, the three had become so close that Becky had come back to school with them for the winter.

Last autumn it had seemed like a perfect solution, Becky thought with a sigh, but this year was different. It was going to be a long, cold winter living in Alison's big stone house by the Hudson River with Alison like a black cloud, fighting her parents every step of the way.

Becky took her bridle off its hook and started for the tack room door just in time to see Alison stomp into the barn, her face slammed shut like a book. 'I'm not riding at all today, then,' she shouted over her shoulder to her mother. 'If you don't like it, that's too bad.' She strode down the central hall of the barn to her horse Duchess's stall and disappeared inside.

Becky exchanged a worried glance with Meg. What would happen now? They could hear Alison's mother talking to the stable owner in a low voice. 'I don't know what I'm going to do with her, Virginia. Robert and I are thinking of selling Duchess.'

Now the look Becky and Meg shared was one

of horror. Sell Duchess! Alison might be spoiled and difficult, she might rebel against her mother's constant demands to win trophies, but she loved her beautiful champion mare.

The stable owner's voice was equally low, but calmer. 'She's a lovely horse.'

'Yes, and she deserves the kind of rider who will put her best effort into winning, not someone who can't be bothered half the time.'

'I'm sure Alison does her best,' they heard Virginia murmur.

'That's just it.' Marion Chant's voice had an icy edge. 'She absolutely does not do her best. The horse is worth over fifty thousand dollars. It's not a good investment if Alison is not going to take competition seriously.'

'Development in dressage has its plateaus. Like every other kind of learning,' they could hear Virginia say.

'Of course, but this has nothing to do with a learning plateau. Alison's attitude is the problem.

We see it at home, in a thousand ways. She's lazy, rude and inconsiderate. I don't know what we're going to do with her!' There was a pause. 'I haven't decided yet, but if you hear of anyone looking for a good dressage horse, I hope you'll let me know.'

The two voices moved out of earshot. Becky and Meg gaped at each other. 'She wouldn't really sell Duchess?' Meg's blue eyes were troubled.

'She might.' Becky made a face. 'She might just do it to punish Alison.'

Alone with her horse, Alison took a couple of deep breaths, not wanting to frighten Duchess with her anger and frustration. 'How are you, old girl?' she whispered, leaning her head against Duchess's warm horse-fragrant cheek.

Duchess blew softly through her great nostrils and tossed her head gently, as if to answer. She was a big horse, almost sixteen hands and strongly built, a Dutch warmblood. Alison knew she was lucky to have such a magnificent animal, but it wasn't Duchess's breeding and training she loved, it was the way Duchess nickered a 'hello' when she saw her, followed her in the paddock without being led, and seemed to know how she was feeling, like now.

'My mother thinks I don't try,' Alison whispered, brushing Duchess's forelock back and massaging the small white blaze on her forehead. But we know better, don't we, Dutch?' She remembered with a spurt of bitter anger, how it had been at that last dressage event. Duchess had not been feeling her best. As soon as Alison mounted her, she could feel that the mare was slightly 'off', not really sick, but just not able to focus. She knew, right then, they weren't going to win, so instead of pushing the big horse, she just lay back, gave her some slack and decided to enjoy the day.

They'd done a respectable job, and came fifth.

But, of course, that wasn't good enough for her mother!

Alison reached in her kit bag for a soft brush and began to gently brush Duchess's glossy hide in circular strokes. It soothed the anger she felt remembering her mother's scorching words after the results were announced. It was no use telling her Duchess hadn't been feeling her best. 'You have to push her!' Marion Chant had raged in front of everybody. 'She's not a pet, she's a champion, and you have to make her be her best at all times, not just when she wants to win. Haven't I taught you anything?'

Yes, Alison thought bitterly, working her brush down Duchess's flank. You've taught me winning is the only thing that matters. This summer, out at Mustang Mountain Ranch, she'd learned that other things were important – such as being kind to Duchess when she wasn't at the top of her form. That new Alison had struggled to stay alive for a few weeks after they got back. But she could feel herself sinking into her mother's world again, where status and being the best were the only things that mattered.

'Sometimes, I really hate her,' Alison whispered to Duchess, ducking under her neck to brush her other side. 'If only Dad would take my side.' But her father was worried about business these days, and he and her mother were constantly battling. He seemed to have no time to even listen to her problems.

'If you're not riding, we're going home,' she heard her mother's voice say. 'I'm not wasting time while you sulk!' She looked up to see her mother's angry face.

'What about Becky's lesson?' Alison threw up her chin and faced her mother.

'She'll have to miss it.'

'That's not fair . . .' Alison flared.

'Well, you should have thought of that! Is it fair that I interrupt my day to drive you all the way out here for nothing?' They glared at each other, neither giving in, then Alison turned away with a careless shrug.

'Goodbye, Dutch,' she murmured, kissing Duchess on the side of her head, and giving her face a last rub. 'See you Thursday.'

Meg watched the black Porsche turn down the stable drive towards the river and speed through the gate on to the main road. Meg could walk home from Blue Barns, but Alison and Becky lived on the other side of town, further along the Hudson River.

Meg turned back into the barn and walked down the row of stalls, stopping to rub the faces of the horses and working her way towards Duchess. The first time Meg had met Alison she was riding Duchess, right here at Blue Barns, and Meg had been awestruck at the picture of them. A perfect vision of a girl on a horse, like the kind of thing Meg had been reading about and dreaming about since she was a little kid.

She stopped at Duchess's stall and the big horse thrust her nose out in greeting. 'Here, girl, I can at least turn you out and muck out your stall.' She gave the aristocratic nose a pat. 'I'd exercise you, too, if I didn't think Alison's mom would have a fit!' Alison would have done that, if she'd stayed. One of the best things about Alison was the way she loved her horse. Meg could no more imagine her without Duchess than . . . than myself without Silver, she thought with a pang and a shake of her long brown ponytail.

Silver was gone. The gangly white colt she'd rescued in a snowstorm, the beautiful horse she'd loved and nursed back to health, had gone – back to his home stable in Maryland. For over a year she had looked after him, loved him, helped his leg heal after an accident. It had been almost like having her own horse. Almost, but

Meg had known that she couldn't keep Silver, and she was glad he was ready to begin his training as a jumper.

She just hadn't counted on how much she'd miss him.

She clipped a lead rope to Duchess's halter, opened the stall and led the tall chestnut to the wide doors at the other end of the barn. Some day I will have my own horse, Meg thought. I'll get a job and save every cent and find the perfect horse.

The vision of a red mustang, galloping across a mountain meadow, leaped into her mind. On his back was Thomas, the boy who had captured this wild horse to be the foundation of his herd. Meg sighed. Thomas and his mustang stallion were far away in the Rockies. Someday, she might see them again. In the meantime, she could help out at Blue Barns and earn enough to help pay for her lessons, and spend her time with the school horses and the boarders, like Duchess.

'They couldn't sell you.' The sunlight gleamed on Duchess's smooth hide, as glossy and bright as a new chestnut. 'You belong here.'

Sky Horse

How could Becky's parents dump her on this wilderness ranch where there was no town, no kids her own age, no paved roads?

Becky and her parents have moved into the wild to Mustang Mountain. Soon cousin Alison from the city and her mad-about-horses friend Meg will arrive for the summer. The girls will have to overcome their differences as they battle an unexpected snowstorm, rescue a young adventurer from his crashed plane, and come face to face with a grizzly bear.

Step into the wild as drama and danger await at Mustang Mountain.

Fire Horse

'It's far away, nothin' to worry about. We get wildfires almost every year out here in the Rockies.'

During the summer Becky begins to lose her fear of horses, Meg is busy with her horse, Silver; and Alison can't stop thinking about Jesse, the tall cowboy with those gorgeous dark blue eyes.

When an accident puts Becky's mother in hospital, the girls are left alone on the Mustang Mountain Ranch. Then two horses go missing and the girls set out on a rescue mission, but a wild stallion threatens their plans. All the while a wildfire rages, putting the girls at great risk.

Step into the wild as drama and danger await at Mustang Mountain.

Wild Horse

'I don't want another horse.' Alison tossed back her hair. *'If I can't have Duchess, I'm never riding again.'*

Becky, Alison and Meg are spending a week on a ranch in Wyoming. Becky and Meg are thrilled by the promise of riding wild horses, but Alison can't stop thinking about her father selling her horse, Duchess. Everything seems to be going wrong until Alison discovers a sick mare that needs her help. With the help of good-looking Josh, Alison puts her plan into place. But can she save the mare before it's too late?

Step into the wild as drama and danger await at Mustang Mountain.

Rodeo Horse

In a few minutes, it would be too late for anyone to see her from the road. It would be dark.

When Alison moves to Horner Creek, she discovers the excitement of the rodeo. Becky is busy struggling to train the wild horse Shadow, and finding out about the secretive boy Rob. And poor Meg is stuck in New York, longing to join her friends.

An accident unites the girls, and they must work together to find out whether it really was an accident.

Step into the wild as drama and danger await at Mustang Mountain.

Brave Horse

*Hoof beats pounded down the streambed. A huge black
animal came thundering out of the fog . . .*

Becky, Alison and Meg are back at Mustang
Mountain Ranch . . . and they are surrounded by
danger. The girls hear about a phantom black
stallion, and then Thomas goes missing in
pursuit of the legendary horse. The girls organise
a rescue party . . . but Alison's hiding something
from her friends that could jeopardise the
mission. And then there's the curse of the ghost
horse . . . will it thwart their plans?

Step into the wild as drama and danger await at
Mustang Mountain.

EGMONT PRESS: ETHICAL PUBLISHING

Egmont Press is about turning writers into successful authors and children into passionate readers – producing books that enrich and entertain. As a responsible children's publisher, we go even further, considering the world in which our consumers are growing up.

Safety First
Naturally, all of our books meet legal safety requirements. But we go further than this; every book with play value is tested to the highest standards – if it fails, it's back to the drawing-board.

Made Fairly
We are working to ensure that the workers involved in our supply chain – the people that make our books – are treated with fairness and respect.

Responsible Forestry
We are committed to ensuring all our papers come from environmentally and socially responsible forest sources.

**For more information, please visit our website at
www.egmont.co.uk/ethical**